DO YOU GET INTO ARGUMENTS?

Do You Get Into Arguments?

Monique Vescia and
Karen Judson

Enslow Publishing
101 W. 23rd Street
Suite 240
New York, NY 10011
USA
enslow.com

Published in 2016 by Enslow Publishing, LLC.
101 W. 23rd Street, Suite 240, New York, NY 10011

Library of Congress Cataloging-in-Publication Data

Vescia, Monique.
Do you get into arguments? / Monique Vescia and Karen Judson.
pages cm. — (Got issues?)
Audience: Grade 9 to 12.
Includes bibliographical references and index.
Summary: "Describes difficulties facing teens today concerning anger, misunderstandings, and tempers"— Provided by publisher.
ISBN 978-0-7660-7189-6
1. Anger—Juvenile literature. 2. Temper—Juvenile literature. 3. Miscommunication. I. Judson, Karen, 1941– II. Title.
BF575.A5V47 2016
155.5'1247—dc23

2015028086

Printed in the United States of America

To Our Readers: We have done our best to make sure all websites in this book were active and appropriate when we went to press. However, the author and the publisher have no control over and assume no liability for the material available on those websites or on any websites they may link to. Any comments or suggestions can be sent by e-mail to customerservice@enslow.com.

Portions of this book originally appeared in the book *Resolving Conflicts: How to Get Along When You Don't Get Along.*

Disclaimer: For many of the images in this book, the people photographed are models. The depictions do not imply actual situations or events.

Photo Credits: Cover, p. 3 Gelpi JM/Shutterstock.com; p. 7 Stockbyte/Thinkstock; p. 8, 28 Monkey Business Images/Shutterstock; p. 11 Jan Tyler/iStock/Thinkstock; p. 22 © AP Images; p. 25 Morton Broffman/Archive Photos/Getty Images; p. 31 Catherine Yeulet/iStock/Thinkstock; p. 32 Highwaystarz-Photography/iStock/Thinkstock; p. 34 Jupiterimages/Creatas/Thinkstock; p. 39 © iStockphoto.com/caracterdesign; p. 41 Sabphoto/Shutterstock.com; p.43 Kzenon/Shutterstock.com ; p. 45 © iStockphoto.com/Rob Mattingley; p. 46 oliveromg/Shutterstock.com; p. 51 © Ace Stock Limited/Alamy; p. 54 © iStockphoto.com/Steve Debenport; p. 58 © iStockphoto.com/sturti; p. 63 Odd Andersen/AFP/Getty Images; p. 66 Time Life Pictures/Mansell/The LIFE Picture Collection/Getty Images; p. 69 Jennifer Bruce/AFP/Getty Images; p. 73 AP Photo/The Daily Reflector, Jenni Farrow; p. 79 Photographee.eu/Shutterstock.com; p. 82 Susan Biddle/The Washington Post/Getty Images; p. 84 © David Young-Wolff / PhotoEdit; p. 86 © iStockphoto.com/franckreporter; p. 90 Purestock/Thinkstock; p.93 @erics/Shutterstock.com; p. 95 Andrei Jackamets / © Bravo / Courtesy: Everett Collection;
p. 97 Photofusion/Universal Images Group via Getty Images; p. 100 Nicole Weiss/Shutterstock.com;
p. 102 Sylvie Bouchard/Shutterstock.com; p. 104 RypeArts/Shutterstock.com; p. 107 Gail Hardy/iStock/Thinkstock; p. 109 Stokkete/Shutterstock.com.

Contents

Some of the names in this book are fictional, but the stories come out of the author's own experience as a parent and teacher. All of the words, feelings, and situations described are based on real people's experiences with conflict and conflict resolution.

1

Defining Conflict

Do you find yourself getting into arguments with your friends and family or even strangers? When something doesn't go your way, do you take it out on those around you? Do you have trouble dealing with people whose opinions differ from yours? Do you pick fights? If so, you may find that you have trouble with conflict.

What is conflict? It may be as minor as two bargain hunters squabbling over the same item on a sale rack or as major as two nations going to war. Sometimes conflicts begin over something insignificant and balloon into something far more serious. Most people experience some degree of conflict every day. As a teenager, you may feel like you've had more than your share. Chances are you often find yourself in a conflict with a parent, teacher, sibling, or even with a best friend.

Imagine the following conflict scenarios:

- You found out that one of your friends is dating the guy who just broke up with you, and you feel betrayed by both your friend and your ex-boyfriend.
- Your parents refuse to let you go camping with a group of your friends because the group consists of both boys and girls, and you are angry because you think your parents do not trust you.
- It is frustrating that even though you have just earned your driver's license, your father will not let you take the car by yourself.

Do you get into arguments with your parents? Conflicts can arise when children and parents have different ideas. Maybe you disagree about your curfew or the amount of your allowance.

- You have been looking forward to the prom for months, but now it is only two weeks away and your boss will not give you time off.
- A customer where you work blames you—unjustly and loudly—for shortchanging her.
- For the third time this month your girlfriend stands you up.
- You got a ticket for speeding that you feel you did not deserve, and when you tried to talk the police officer out of it, he got angry.
- A friend invited you to see a movie, but you lied and said your parents would not let you go. The truth was that you thought someone you have a crush on was going to ask you to the same movie, and you wanted to be free to accept that invitation. The person you lied to now seems to dislike you, and you feel guilty.

Everyone experiences conflict—from the president of the United States (of course, his or her job is handling conflicts) to kids in kindergarten (remember when you and another five-year-old fought furiously over the crayon you both wanted?).

Conflicts can arise as we interact with strangers, family members, employers, authority figures, acquaintances, friends, members of groups we belong to, and others. Maybe you and your parents do not agree on your choice of friends. Or perhaps the basketball team you play on cannot agree on which player to elect as team captain. Some conflicts cause a stronger emotional response than others. It would probably be more difficult, for example, to resolve a conflict with your parents over your choice of friends than to decide which teammate to elect.

We tend to think of any kind of conflict as hurtful, but a personal conflict is not always wrong and does not always involve an angry confrontation. A life totally without conflict might sound desirable, but it would most likely become boring.

Life is interesting because it is filled with surprises, expectations, disappointment, and conflict. On the other hand, sometimes conflicts lead to hostility and worse, and if not resolved, they can make life miserable for everyone involved.

There is no doubt that conflict creates challenges, but conflict does not mean that a fight is unavoidable or the individuals involved will become enemies. The key to successfully meeting challenges and growing in the process is learning how to handle conflict. Consider the following example:

Fourteen-year-old Brian and his twelve-year-old sister, Emily, live on a twenty-acre ranch outside Denver, Colorado. When they recently moved out of the city to the ranch, they each wanted a horse, but their parents told them that they would have to help buy the horses. Their parents would pay for hay, veterinary bills, and tack, but the two siblings would have to pay at least half of the purchase price for the horses. Brian and Emily pooled their savings but could not manage half of the price of two saddle horses. "We have enough money for one horse, so let's buy one horse together," Emily suggested, "and we'll both ride it."

"Good idea," Brian agreed. "We'll save our allowances and any money we earn until we have enough for a second horse."

The plan sounded workable, and the two bought a horse they both liked. The thing Brian and Emily had not anticipated, however, was the conflict that arose when they wanted to ride the horse at the same time. For instance, Emily had a slumber party and her three guests wanted to ride Beau, the new gelding. But that same evening, Brian brought four friends home after school and they, too, were eager to ride Beau.

Emily was the first to get to the horse, and she helped one of her friends mount before Brian could intervene.

"You're such a brat, Emily," Brian shouted. "By the time you and your friends finish, it will be too late for me and my friends."

"I'm telling mom you called me a brat." Emily stormed into the house with her friends in tow.

It's easy to get on each others' nerves when you are siblings living in the same house. Brothers and sisters get into arguments all the time about borrowing the car and preferential treatment from parents.

A compromise was arranged in which each of Brian's friends would alternate with each of Emily's friends for a twenty-minute ride. No one was entirely satisfied with the arrangement, however. The rides were too short, Brian and Emily continued to argue, and the horse was nervous over the frequent changes in riders and nearly dislodged a couple of his passengers. It was apparent after all the guests went home that some sort of structured, mutually acceptable arrangement would be necessary if the horse co-ownership was to work.

Clearly, Brian and Emily were in the middle of a conflict that would have to be resolved before they could enjoy their shared horse.

How Is Conflict Defined?

The dictionary defines conflict as:

- A fight or battle
- Competitive or opposing action
- An antagonistic state or action
- A mental struggle

Conflicts are clashes or disagreements between or among individuals, members of a group, or nations. (When nations fail at conflict resolution, wars or military actions can result.) Conflicts can also be internal—occurring within yourself. This can happen for many reasons, such as when you feel torn between your feelings and what you or others see as the right behavior in a situation. An example of this was mentioned in the chapter opening, where a person lies to a friend then feels guilty. Internal conflicts often arise when you need to make a decision and you cannot decide. Your mother chooses your clothes for you, but she doesn't know what's cool. You wish she would stop, but if you tell her she will be hurt and angry. Three of the colleges you apply to have accepted you, and now you have to decide which one to attend.

Every individual has beliefs, values, goals, behavior patterns, needs, wants, interests, and opinions that are unique to that individual. The individuals that make up a nation have collective customs, habits, and religious and political views, as well, that make them distinct from people in other nations. It is not surprising, therefore, that when individuals or nations interact, these unique characteristics sometimes collide, or when individuals act contrary to deeply rooted values, they feel internally conflicted.

Sources of Conflict

Individuals become involved in conflicts when beliefs, goals, and interests clash or when needs are not met. According to Tim Ursiny, a counselor who works as a success coach and author of *The Coward's Guide to Conflict: Empowering Solutions for Those Who Would Rather Run Than Fight*, people most often experience conflict over differences in perspective (the way we see situations) and differences in beliefs, actions, or interests. "Sometimes these differences are verbalized and sometimes they are not," Ursiny writes, "but either way conflict exists."[1] For example:

1. You differ with someone over *perspective*: A new student in your school "steals" your best friend. You become angry with the newcomer and see her as too pushy and insensitive. As you get to know the new student, however, you are surprised to learn that she sees herself as friendly and outgoing and had no idea that you see her as an intruder.
2. Your *beliefs* differ from those of someone else: A close relative dies and someone you thought was his friend cannot attend your relative's memorial service because of religious beliefs about attending a service in a church not of his denomination. You no longer feel friendly toward your relative's friend.

3. A clash occurs over differences in *goals* and *interests*: Brian and Emily, co-owners of a horse, fought over differences in personal goals and interests. Differences in goals and interests often arise over control issues. For example, both Brian and Emily believed they had the right to control who would ride the horse and when it would be ridden, and neither was willing to hand over control to the other. The horse was caught in the middle, as both Brian's and Emily's friends waited for turns to ride, and the animal acted out the nervousness he felt. Had one of the riders been hurt, the conflict might have expanded to include the parents of Brian's and Emily's guests.

Sometimes all of the above issues are present in a conflict. For example, the conflict in the Middle East that is so often in the news involves two homelands—Israel and Palestine—that have been fighting for decades. Israel was created out of Palestine in 1948 to give the Jewish people a place of their own to settle after World War II. A simplified version of the conflict is that the Palestinians have long been unhappy about giving up land for a Jewish settlement, and both nations want a section of land for their own that includes the ancient city of Jerusalem. Neither side is willing to give up more land or control of the area to the other. The conflict is further fueled by the fact that the Israelis and Palestinians have differing belief systems, since the Israelis are largely Jewish and the Palestinians are predominately Muslim. Israeli and Palestinian Christians also live in the area. No permanent solution has yet been found, and thousands of people on both sides have been wounded or died during the years of fighting.

Different Kinds of Conflict

Conflicts have been categorized in many different ways. Some sources classify conflicts according to those involved:

1. **Intrapersonal:** A conflict felt within one's self. For example, assume you have secretly witnessed a bullying incident near school where the victim was seriously injured. You want to tell the authorities what you saw but are afraid the bully will find out and come after you.

2. **Interpersonal:** A conflict between or among two or more people. Your parents have recently divorced, and it was not a friendly parting. The two hostile adults cannot agree on anything, including division of belongings or custody arrangements for you and your brothers and sisters.

3. **Intragroup:** A conflict that arises when two or more members of the same group disagree. You are a member of the school chorus, and the group presents an annual performance fund-raiser. This year, half the musicians want to present an evening of classical music, and the other half is opposed. Instead, they want to perform popular music—primarily rock and rap.

4. **Intergroup:** A conflict that arises when two or more groups disagree. The school administration allows all extracurricular groups to present budgetary needs at an annual meeting with the student council. The groups equally divide a small amount of money provided by the school board, but this year some groups insist they need a bigger share than other groups. The meeting ends hopelessly deadlocked with some group members insulting others. Groups that have worked together in the past are now vowing never to cooperate again.[2]

It is not uncommon for a conflict to begin as intrapersonal or interpersonal and then to include more individuals, as in the following example. The concert band is traveling on a school bus to another city for a music festival. Alicia and Brandy sit together.

Justine and Clarice share the seat ahead of the two girls, and the four are talking. Alicia has previously admitted to the group of girls that she likes Troy, who plays drums in the band. Clarice also secretly likes Troy (this is the intrapersonal conflict), and she chooses a quiet moment on the bus to remark loudly, "Hey, everyone, Alicia likes Troy." (Now the conflict has become interpersonal.) Troy, who is sitting in the back of the bus, blushes as the boys sitting next to him tease him.

Alicia is mortified and shouts, "Clarice, shut up and mind your own business." Brandy immediately takes Alicia's side, "Geez, Clarice, that was not cool." Justine likes Clarice and sides with her. Soon the other band members on the bus are choosing sides. The conflict between Alicia and Clarice has escalated to include other band members (an intragroup conflict). Both girls are embarrassed, and by the end of the day, Clarice considers quitting band.

Another way of categorizing conflicts is by the source of the conflict:

1. **Relationship Conflicts.** Relationship conflicts occur between or among individuals with strong ties, such as in families, close friendships, or romantic relationships. When strong negative emotions (for example, anger, jealousy, or resentment), misperceptions, stereotypes, poor communication, or negative behaviors intrude on a close relationship, conflict often results. For example, if an adult family member seeks a romantic relationship outside of the marriage or if a child becomes addicted to drugs, the affected family is headed for conflict.

2. **Data Conflicts.** Data is information. Data conflicts occur when people lack the information they need to make wise decisions or when they are misinformed. For instance, assume you are taking a test in class and you believe the person next to you is looking at answers she has hidden under her hand. You report the cheater to the teacher only to learn that she was not cheating at all. The person you wrongly assumed was cheating now dislikes you and seems bent on making your life miserable.

3. **Interest Conflicts.** Interest conflicts arise when there is competition for a prize or goal that cannot be shared. For example, James is running for president of the student council against Sharon. Both have 3.5 grade point averages and are good public speakers, friendly, outgoing, and interested in a variety of school issues. Obviously, only one student can be elected president, and a vicious name-calling campaign battle takes place that makes James and Sharon enemies for the rest of the school year.
4. **Structural Conflicts.** Structural conflicts are caused by forces outside the control of the people who become involved. For example, a new superintendent is hired in your school district, and he and the school board extend the school day by half an hour—a decision that angers most students and several teachers. Or you have always helped your school's theater group with scenery design, but a new theater arts teacher chooses someone else to design scenery, and you are angry over his decision.
5. **Value Conflicts.** We all have strong opinions about what is good or bad, right or wrong, just or unjust. These opinions represent our values, which are formed mostly from family, religious, and cultural influences. When other people attempt to force their value systems on us or vice versa, conflict is guaranteed. A glaring example is the war pitting the United States against Middle Eastern Islamic terrorists who reject Western culture and its influence on their lives and their countries.[3]

Components of Conflict

Maybe you have a variety of friends who are different from you and each other. Your circle of friends, for example, might include a shy, quiet boy; an outgoing, loud-talking girl; a meticulous, organized person; an untidy individual; a girlfriend who practices a religion different from yours; a boyfriend whose parents are wealthy and provide luxuries you do not have; a girlfriend who comes from a large family in which money is tight; and so on.

On the other hand, maybe you are uncomfortable with people who are different from you. One important component in conflicts is difference. Conflicts often involve differences in goals, needs, values, beliefs, perceptions, religion, gender (such as the way girls and boys are treated), age, social class, nationality, sexual orientation, and many other factors. Here are some examples of how differences can cause conflict.

You assume that all members of certain groups who believe or act differently than you do have nothing in common with you, and therefore, you dislike or distrust them based solely on this wrong assumption. For example, maybe students from the Middle East enroll in your school, and you assume that they all hate Americans, so you make no attempt to get acquainted or include them in your group of friends.

Similarly, have you ever avoided someone you did not know well because he or she seemed stuck up? Perhaps you discovered later, after you got to know this person better, that he or she was not stuck up at all but was simply shy. People often make wrong assumptions about different individuals or groups before they know the person or situation.

In addition to differences, other elements that contribute to conflicts include but are not limited to the following:

Disagreements. When you express your opinion or preferences and they disagree with someone else's opinions or preferences, conflict may result. The the most recent presidential election, for example, was an occasion for voters on Republican and Democratic sides to air their differences. Some disagreements were more heated than others, but conflict was definitely part of the process. This was resolved, for the most part, by election results, but it is ongoing in many individuals who wound up on the losing side of the vote.

Problems. These are another aspect of conflict because differences and disagreements can cause problems. Everyone's daily life involves problems that may or may not be resolved. When problems are ongoing and difficult to resolve, it often helps for the involved parties to discuss the matter with counselors or experts in conflict resolution.

Unresolved problems often lead to disputes where parties have recognized that there is a problem and at least one party wants to resolve the problem. A dispute escalates to a conflict when parties on both sides want to win. Unfortunately, unresolved conflicts where both parties are determined to win can lead to violence, as winning at any cost becomes the goal. The violence can be psychological, emotional, or physical.

The Benefits of Conflict

Any conflict resulting in violence is destructive. This includes conflicts where wars are fought, physical fighting results, or people who disagree with prevailing thought are punished or ostracized.

On the other hand, conflicts that are managed well can have positive outcomes. In *Reducing School Violence Through Conflict Resolution,* authors David W. Johnson and Roger T. Johnson list the following benefits for students who are able to constructively manage conflicts:

- They experience improved achievement, reasoning, and problem solving.
- They become more mature.
- They are better able to understand another person's point of view.
- They learn about themselves—what makes them angry, what frightens them, and what is important to them.
- They are more confident, so they become more cooperative and involved.
- Their psychological health is improved.
- They learn self-reliance and self-discipline.
- They are better able to handle stress and adversity.[4]

"Conflicts make us aware of problems that need to be solved," Johnson and Johnson add. "Recognizing that a problem exists, who is involved, and how we can solve it helps reduce the irritations of relating to others."[5]

The Art of Conflict Resolution

To resolve a conflict means to settle a disagreement with another person, group, or within one's self. Conflict resolution refers to a set of techniques used to reach a satisfactory agreement between or among opposing parties when a conflict exists. There are many options for conflict resolution. You can run away from a conflict, intimidate your opponent with violence, talk the problem out with your opponent, request that a neutral third party hear both sides of the argument, or in some situations, file a lawsuit.

When opponents in a conflict try to solve the problem without going to court, the process is called alternative dispute resolution, a term used in Title 9 of the US Code that establishes federal law for supporting alternatives to filing a court suit. Mediation and arbitration are alternative dispute resolution methods that can, in some cases, be used instead of settling civil cases in court. Civil cases are those in which one party sues another; they do not involve crimes. The court often orders the losing party in a civil suit to pay a certain amount of money to the winning party. Criminal cases involve crimes against the state and are not resolved by arbitration or mediation.

Mediation and arbitration both involve a neutral third party who is especially trained in alternative dispute resolution. Mediators and arbitrators may or may not be attorneys. Mediators and arbitrators gather information, define the issues for people in conflict, and help the involved parties develop options for solving the problems that caused the conflict in the first place. After a solution is agreed upon, mediators and arbitrators help the parties devise an agreement that both will sign. The difference between mediators and arbitrators is that mediators have no decision-making powers, but arbitrators do.

Arbitrators issue a decision that is binding on both parties involved in the dispute. Some states require that certain types of disagreements be arbitrated—for example, some types of credit card disputes and medical complaints—instead of litigated in court.

Conflict Resolution Throughout History

Conflict resolution is a general term used to describe a process that has been around for centuries. Histories of China, Japan, and some African countries tell of villages using peer mediation to solve disputes among residents long before formal conflict resolution methods were used in the United States. In fact, mediation has proved so effective throughout history that it continues to be an accepted method of peacefully resolving conflicts.

About forty years ago, school administrators saw the value in teaching students to resolve conflicts peacefully, and school-based programs were developed. Currently some schools teach conflict resolution to all students as part of the curriculum, while others train specially selected students as peer mediators who can help fellow students resolve conflicts. National peer mediation programs for schools include the following:

- Teaching Students to Be Peacemakers, which was developed by David Johnson and other researchers in the mid-1960s at the University of Minnesota.
- The Children's Creative Response to Conflict program, which was developed in 1972 by Quaker teachers in New York City and became incorporated as Creative Response to Conflict in 1992. The program helps students, teachers, and parents learn peaceful ways to successfully resolve conflicts.
- Peers Making Peace uses a preventative approach for handling problems in and out of school. Each participating school selects a representative group of fifteen to twenty-four students to train as peer mediators. Expulsion rates decreased by 73 percent in schools that adopted the program.[6]

There are many ways of resolving conflict and defusing arguments in the school setting. One is forming a representative group to discuss sources of conflict and find peaceful resolutions.

- SMARTteam (Students Managing Anger and Resolutions Together) is a multimedia computer-based violence prevention program designed for sixth through ninth graders. Introduced in 2006, the software uses games, graphics, cartoons, and interactive interviews to teach conflict-resolution skills.
- Operation Respect was started in 2000 by folksinger Peter Yarrow, a member of the 1960s folksinging trio Peter, Paul, and Mary. The program uses music to bring students together and teaches ways to resolve conflict through classroom activities. The program's focus is the song "Don't Laugh at Me," and the organization offers free educational resources designed to help reduce "the emotional and physical cruelty some children inflict upon each other by behaviors such as ridicule, bullying, and—in extreme cases—violence."[7]

One School's Example

One approach to conflict resolution that has proved effective in school situations is called restorative justice. Many high schools plagued by violence adopted zero tolerance policies that required students who start fights with other students to be suspended from school or expelled. Ultimately, high rates of school suspensions contributed to rising dropout rates and didn't address the roots of the problem.

Some schools, such as the Ralph J. Bunche Academy in Oakland, California, decided to try a different approach. Rather than removing students from school for fighting, the restorative justice model brings them together to talk about their issues face-to-face. With the help of a mediator, who may be an adult or a peer, the students talk it out, tell each other why they are angry, explain their actions, and try to see things from the other person's point of view. The goal of restorative justice is to repair the damage caused by conflicts rather than to punish and exclude the students involved.

Oakland ranks as one of the most violent cities in the United States. Many students at Ralph J. Bunche have experienced traumatic experiences in their neighborhoods and in their homes. Students who drop out of school often join gangs or turn to crime. Educators were determined to find ways to shut down the school-to-prison pipeline. Restorative justice helped to cut the number of suspensions at Ralph J. Bunche Academy by half.[8]

Peacemaking Leads to Progress

Historical records worldwide are full of examples of conflicts that were resolved through courage, perseverance, and peaceful objection to the status quo. Here are a few examples of large-scale conflicts that resulted in positive change:

- The debate between the Federalists and anti-Federalists in eighteenth-century America that led to the Bill of Rights.
- Mahatma Gandhi's peaceful opposition to the British government's discriminatory treatment of people in Africa and India that led to independence for India in 1947.
- Martin Luther King Jr.'s nonviolent persistence in demanding equal civil rights for African Americans in the United States that led to the Civil Rights Act of 1964.
- The successful negotiation over a period of two years—1985 to 1987—between President Ronald Reagan and the USSR's General Secretary Mikhail Gorbachev for a mutual nuclear arms reduction treaty.
- The ongoing efforts of former US President Jimmy Carter (1977–1981) to promote freedom, democracy, and human rights around the world that won him the Nobel Peace Prize in 2002. Among his well-known efforts to promote peace are the Camp David Accords, which were history-making agreements signed by Egyptian President Anwar Sadat and Israeli Prime Minister Menachem Begin in 1978. Camp David is the presidential retreat located in Frederick County, Maryland, near Washington, D.C. Carter had long wanted to help bring peace to the Middle East, and the Camp David Accords were

One of US history's great leaders, Martin Luther King Jr., used peaceful protest to fight for civil rights in the 1960s. Peacemaking is one way to approach conflicts.

noteworthy for getting the Egyptian and Israeli leaders to sit down together to talk. Unfortunately, the accords did not lead to a lasting peace between Palestine and Israel.

Goals of Conflict Resolution

There are many types of and reasons for conflict, but fortunately there are also ways to resolve conflict without fighting, making enemies, or feeling that you are always giving in to others. Compromise, negotiation, and collaboration are methods of conflict resolution that determine the needs of all individuals involved in a dispute and work to satisfy those needs peacefully. To resolve conflicts satisfactorily, the parties involved need to be skillful listeners and truthful communicators. These skills can be learned, and they are discussed in more detail in following chapters.

Some people come naturally to conflict resolution because they were raised in an environment where resolving conflicts by talking with and listening to others was the norm. Others may have been raised in environments where conflicts were never truly resolved but were temporarily handled by aggression, force, running away, or by simply ignoring the problem. Whatever your background or present methods of handling conflict, this book will help you to do the following:

1. Think differently about conflict. Instead of seeing conflict as a fight with someone with one side winning and the other losing, you can learn to see it as a challenge that can be creatively resolved. Everyone involved can feel that he or she has won something, that this is a win-win situation, that it leaves all parties satisfied.
2. Learn that no matter how hopelessly deadlocked a conflict seems, there are ways to settle it peacefully and satisfactorily.
3. Explore the many ways of resolution so you are aware of options open to you when you experience conflict.
4. Become a person who automatically thinks of ways to resolve conflicts with dignity and integrity so none of the individuals involved feels like a loser.
5. Learn how to practice conflict resolution when you need to so that conflicts don't get you down and destroy relationships you value.[9]

Conflict resolution skills will not only help you preserve relationships, they will also earn you the respect of others and ensure that you can successfully settle a disagreement while maintaining your self-respect and peace of mind.

2 Arguments Happen

Life is full of arguments—they're a reality of being human. Every day of your life, as long as you interact with others, you will face conflicts. And when we're not in disagreement with others, we often fight with ourselves.

- Getting up early to go to school may be a conflict because going to bed at a reasonable hour at night is also a conflict.
- Maybe your boss wants you to work an hour longer at your part-time job instead of quitting at your usual time. You don't want to, but you don't have a good excuse not to. You don't want to risk offending your boss and possibly losing your job.
- Suppose a good friend is having a party and you really want to go. However, you and your dad have tickets to a football game that same night, so you will have to make a difficult choice. If you skip the party, you are afraid your friend will be mad at

you, but if you turn down the football game, your father will be disappointed.

- Perhaps you are a member of your school's student council and a motion is made that you don't like, but your arguments go unheard and the motion passes.
- A girl you consider a close friend does not answer when you speak to her in the hallway between classes.

And on and on . . .

Whether or not you realize it, you are experienced at handling conflict. If you're not always satisfied with the way you've handled conflicts, however, you can learn how to improve your conflict resolution skills. Conflicts in your life that have been the most worrisome probably share one or more of the following characteristics:

- A disagreement makes you really mad at a parent, sibling, friend, teacher, or someone else.
- You have difficulty going about your daily business because of a disagreement that you have been unable to settle. You cannot eat or sleep, you have become irritable, and your schoolwork is suffering. Bullying often causes these reactions in victims and is discussed later in this resource.
- You have been trying to ignore someone who is harassing you, but it isn't working. Your harasser has constantly teased, berated, and challenged you, and you want it to stop.
- You disagree with an adult authority figure—a teacher, your boss, your parents—over an issue that is important to you. You feel powerless to change the situation, and you fume in silence.
- You realize that making a decision entirely on your own will not successfully resolve a problem. You need to involve the individuals on the other side to remedy the situation.

Ways of Resolving Arguments

Once you determine that you have a conflict with others that requires more than a quick decision to settle, you can decide how to handle it. The method you use to resolve a conflict will probably depend on your goals and how much you value your relationship with the other party. There are several ways, some more constructive than others, to resolve a conflict without resorting to aggression or violence. The best ways to resolve conflicts are usually win-win in nature. That is, they let both sides win something. Here are five basic ways of resolving conflict.[1]

1. **Avoidance or denial**. Walking away from a conflict may be an option if one or more of the following conditions exist:

    - No relationship exists between you and the person with whom you are in conflict.
    - There is a relationship, but it is not important to you to continue it.
    - The conflict is not important to you.
    - The conflict bothers you, but the timing is wrong for a confrontation, and you need a cooling-off period.

    If you can walk away from the conflict without feeling bad, you can consider the conflict resolved—at least from your viewpoint. For example: A large group of striking employees is picketing in front of a store you want to enter. The strikers are aggressive and insist on blocking your way. A classmate of yours is one of the strikers, and he zeroes in on you. You can postpone shopping in that store, or you can go to another store that sells the same products. Since you do not know the striking classmate well, you decide to avoid confronting the strikers and you leave.

Denial is also a form of avoiding conflict. Denying that the conflict exists is not generally an acceptable resolution because it results in a win-lose situation, and chances are the issue will not disappear but will actually build. If you simply deny to yourself that a conflict exists, you will probably continue to feel resentment and anger. For example, when Rebecca's family built a backyard pool, she invited Susan, her best friend, to swim nearly every afternoon after school while the weather was warm. Others soon heard about the pool, however, and Rebecca did not know how to limit swimming guests. Several rowdy boys and girls started showing up to swim. After a few days, Susan was no longer enjoying herself,

Walking away from an argument can be an effective way to deal with conflict, but it is probably not the best thing to do when your parent is trying to talk to you.

so she quit going to Rebecca's house to swim. Rebecca was unhappy with the situation but had no idea how to solve the problem, so she simply denied to herself that it existed. During the next few days, she seldom saw Susan after school, and she was mad at her friend for ignoring her. When Rebecca's mother asked why she seldom saw Susan anymore, Rebecca snapped, "I don't want to talk about it. Leave me alone," and stomped off to her room.

Accommodation is a good tactic when resolving the conflict in your favor is not especially important to you. This can be an effective approach when dealing with elderly family members.

2. **Accommodation**. Giving in to the demands of others is fine if this is your decision and you are happy with the outcome. Some conflict resolution experts call this suppression or smoothing over, however, which is generally not a good way to resolve conflicts because it results in a win-lose outcome and can lead to resentment. In the following example, Charlett accommodates her great-aunt without feeling resentment.

   Charlett's ninety-year-old great-aunt invited the family for brunch every other Sunday. Since her great-aunt believed that girls should wear dresses for special occasions, she would be disappointed and possibly angry if Charlett were to wear slacks or jeans. However, Charlett often left her great-aunt's house to join her friends for a bike ride or some other activity, and dressing up for brunch meant that she had to take a change of clothes. It was inconvenient, but rather than oppose her great-aunt, Charlett took another set of clothes to wear when she left her great-aunt's house. This was an accommodation that Charlett agreed to make to spare her great-aunt's feelings.

   Accommodation is no solution, however, if you do not want to give in to the demands of others or if giving in can have serious emotional or physical consequences for you. For example, Jeffrey developed asthma early in his life, and by the time he was fifteen, his doctor had identified several substances that caused him to have asthma attacks. One such trigger was animal dander. Jeffrey's friends knew about his asthma but had never witnessed one of his asthma attacks. When one of the boys who lived on a ranch invited the group to go horseback riding, they talked Jeffrey into going. "Don't be such a sissy," they chided. "So you'll cough a little for a while. It will be worth it." Jeffrey let himself be persuaded, and as a result, he suffered a serious asthma attack and had to be rushed to the hospital.

3. **Power or dominance.** If the parties involved in a conflict agree to settle the matter by majority rule or agree to let a person in authority solve the problem, the conflict is resolved. This method of settling a conflict can work if involved parties see it as fair and have agreed in advance to use the method. It is also acceptable if the authority who will make the decision is respected and trusted. Disadvantages, however, are that a win-lose situation has been created and that losers may feel ignored or disrespected.

Parents and teens often argue about homework, but one way to avoid an argument over homework is collaboration. Working together will help you with your work and prove your responsibility to your parent.

A mediator may be a trusted adult when teenagers or younger children are involved in a conflict, or he or she may be a student trained in peer mediation. In schools that have a peer mediation program, trained student mediators may be asked to help resolve a conflict that seems hopelessly deadlocked. Peer mediation is discussed in detail later in this resource. In the following example, two students allow a mediator to solve a conflict that grew until it was out of control.

Natalie and Barbara had been best friends in middle school, but when the two girls entered high school, their relationship changed. Natalie was more outgoing than Barbara, and she earned a spot on the cheerleading squad. Barbara had always wanted to be a cheerleader but was too shy to try out. After Natalie became a cheerleader, Barbara was jealous, but instead of voicing her concerns to Natalie, she avoided her former friend. Barbara stewed in silence until she had convinced herself that Natalie was a snob. To retaliate, Barbara told another cheerleader that she thought Natalie was taking drugs.

The rumor soon spread. Natalie heard that Barbara had started the rumor, and she confronted her former friend. Barbara denied that she had spread the story and accused Natalie of being too stuck up for former friends after she became a cheerleader. A teacher heard the girls arguing and suggested they request peer mediation to resolve their differences. Neither girl wanted to bring in a third person, but the teacher convinced them to try mediation. A peer mediator worked with the girls, and while the friendship was not restored to its former closeness, Barbara agreed not to spread any more vicious rumors about Natalie, and Natalie agreed to include Barbara in some of the activities they had shared before Natalie became a cheerleader.

4. **Compromise or negotiation.** Compromise and negotiation are useful when resources are limited, such as in the example of one horse for Brian and Emily to share. This is often the most satisfactory way to resolve a dispute but only if both sides trust and respect each other, have enough leeway to give, and realize that they probably will not get everything they want. Compromise implies that each side in a conflict will have to give up something they want so both sides can come away at least partially satisfied. Some goals on each side of the conflict and some part of a relationship may have to be sacrificed to reach a compromise, but it is still a win-win method of resolving a conflict.

   In the earlier conflict over sharing a horse, Brian and Emily decided on a compromise where Emily and her friends would have sole use of the horse on Saturdays, and Brian and his friends could ride on Sundays. During the week, the co-owners could each ride for one hour but only after homework and chores were done. If either sibling violated the agreement, that person would forfeit all riding privileges for one week. Since the compromise involved limiting riding time for both Brian and Emily, neither got what he or she really wanted—complete control over the horse—but both sides could ride during their specified times without interference. The compromise the two negotiated resolved the conflict, but neither Brian nor Emily got what he or she really wanted, which was the freedom to ride whenever he or she chose.

5. **Collaboration.** Collaboration is a method of conflict resolution that works well when more than two individuals are involved. When members of a group are in conflict with each other but agree on a mutually satisfying resolution, this is collaboration. As in a compromise between two individuals, all parties seldom get everything they want.

As a member of his school's student council, Steven often collaborates with other council representatives to recommend changes to the school administration that students believe will benefit the school. For instance, when a student in Tennessee started a movement to get students to sign wallet-sized pledge cards that they would stop taunting others and would encourage kindness, Steven lobbied his student council members to also adopt the pledge. Some council members thought the pledges would be simply symbolic and therefore ineffective, since there were no enforcement provisions or methods of measuring success. Steven persisted in requesting that students in his school be offered the chance to sign the pledges, and the student council finally agreed to bring the suggestion to school administrators. The administrators liked Steven's idea, and six months after a majority of students had signed the pledges, Steven noticed a difference in his school. "People are nicer to each other," he remarked, "and some kids who had been picked on aren't anymore."

Violent responses to conflicts are, of course, always undesirable. These responses include shouting, name calling, and physical fighting. Less violent but still undesirable responses include rolling the eyes, arguing, being overly critical and unfair, or harassing other individuals involved in the dispute.

How to Get What You Want

In *Getting What You Want: How to Reach Agreement and Resolve Conflict Every Time*, author Kare Anderson emphasizes that the answer to resolving conflict is not to change other people or to show them up as wrong. When the situation heats up, Anderson recommends, use the following four steps to keep resolution on track:

1. Remind yourself that in most conflicts, there are no good and bad guys. Those involved in the conflict may be irritating to each other, but neither side is absolutely right or absolutely wrong.
2. Remember that you may have to take it upon yourself to lower your voice, cool down, and deal rationally with the situation. If you wait for the other side to calm things down, it may never happen.
3. If you feel yourself getting more and more angry, ask yourself why you are reacting so strongly so you can let go.
4. Ask yourself how (or if) the differences between you and the other side can be fixed.[2]

Sometimes controlling a conflict situation means defusing another person's anger, says Gary Harper in *The Joy of Conflict Resolution*. Because anger overrules reason, it is hard to solve any problem when one or both parties are mad. To get started discussing a problem with a person who is shouting, name calling, stomping around, and otherwise showing anger, try these basic tips:

- Give the person a minute to storm without interrupting, then say something such as, "OK, now tell me that again without swearing."
- Create speed bumps. As a person's anger builds, he or she may be incapable of listening for long, but if you simply say the person's name or repeat a key word or two, you may slow the momentum and help the person's anger spiral down.
- Show empathy. When you can get a word in, tell the person that you are trying to understand. "I know how you feel," is sometimes just a red flag that encourages an angry person to tell us no, we do not know how he or she feels. But if you can let the person know that you are truly listening, maybe he or

To keep a conflict from escalating into an argument or a more serious fight, take a minute to breathe, lower the volume of your voice, and listen to the other person's side.

she will begin to calm down. For example, you might say, "I can see that this has really ticked you off" or "It sounds as though you think you're being blamed here."[3]

The above techniques for defusing anger are part of active listening, which is discussed later in this resource.

Although you are not always in complete control of a conflict situation, you are in control of your own behavior. Anderson tells the tale of a man who had bought his morning paper at the same newsstand for many years. The proprietor of the newsstand was always grumpy and unfriendly, but the man continued to say a cheery, "Good morning, Sam," every day and ignore Sam's snarling response. A person who observed this behavior asked the man why he continued to be nice to Sam when he was so unfriendly. The man replied, "Why should I let someone else determine my behavior?"[4]

If you have ever been involved in a conflict that seemed to go on forever and left you sad, angry, and resentful, you know how important it is to learn skills that will help you satisfactorily settle a dispute. Even if you have never experienced the anxiety a hostile conflict can cause, learning conflict resolution skills can help you through life's everyday conflicts.

3 Resolving Conflicts and Reducing Arguments

When arguments are not resolved and hostility simmers, relationships can be destroyed and peace of mind shattered. Conflicts that continue to fester can result in emotional and psychological damage, and physical violence can erupt. The destructive potential of conflict seems to be recognized even among other animals, such as chimpanzees, bottlenose dolphins, domestic dogs, and hyenas. Like human beings, these social animals engage in reconciliation behaviors.[1]

Recognizing Arguments Before They Happen

You may think a conflict with someone else is easy to spot and heated arguments will be the first clue that something is wrong. That is not always the case, however. Remember when a friend did not speak to you for a week and you had no idea why? Or a person quit dating you when you thought the two of you hit it off well? Or when you realized that you no longer had much in common with a longtime friend and the friendship was slipping away? A conflict would not exist in the above situations if no one involved was bothered. The first clue that a conflict exists is when one or both parties is unhappy with a situation and wants it to change. When you know you do not want a situation to continue as it is, it may be time to think about ways to define and resolve the conflict.

What if you want to change a situation and other parties involved seem to think everything is just fine? In that case, consider the following options:

- Ask the other person to meet with you privately.
- In a nonthreatening manner, ask the person if there is a problem. If his or her answer is no, tell the person that you think there is a problem and explain why.
- As you discuss the situation, practice creative listening and ask for feedback. Do not make accusations.
- Try to listen to the other person with an open mind.
- Don't blame the other person.
- Try to work out a compromise that satisfies both of you.[2]

Similarly, sometimes inner conflicts sneak up on us, like that time you wanted to be part of a certain group so much that you shoplifted some gum just to prove you were cool–then felt so conflicted you decided the stunt wasn't worth the guilt trip. You need to get your homework done, but the TV keeps distracting you. You know you should exercise, but it is so easy to be a couch potato. Inner conflicts are with us all the time, and when neglected or allowed to pile up, sometimes they become a more serious problem, called neurosis—a condition that requires professional help and is beyond the scope of this resource.

Conflict cannot always be avoided, but if you can recognize certain signs that a conflict is brewing, you may be able to head it off or at least reduce the impact. For example, what are your personal triggers? Are there words or behaviors that always set you off? Maybe your personal triggers are certain facial expressions, a tone of voice, a pointing finger, or a specific phrase. For example, for Cole, "you always . . ." was a phrase that could turn a minor argument into a fight. "You always make me wait; you always turn things around; you always . . ." No one always does anything, Cole believed, and when someone told him he always did something irritating, he felt like fighting.

You usually can't stop others from raising your irritation meter in the first place, but if you feel your temper rising in response to a trigger, you might walk away, count to ten before responding to give

If you recognize that you're having a conflict with someone, invite the other person for a coffee or a walk and discuss the situation. State your feelings calmly and listen to the other person's point of view.

yourself time to cool off, ignore the remark or behavior (which is hard to do), or—and this choice is doubly hard—if you know the statement is true, you might apologize. For example, if a friend is irritated with you because, "You always make me wait for you," and you know you do tend to run late, you might apologize, and you might also want to make a stronger effort to be on time. The point is, once you recognize your personal triggers, you can better control your emotions, which can lead, in turn, to heading off or resolving an argument.[3]

Another method that often prevents an argument or defuses a brewing conflict is actively listening to others. Trying to get a point across to someone who is not listening is like talking to a wall. It is also discouraging and maddening. You don't like it, and neither does anyone else. On the other hand, active listening shows others you care about what they have to say. Here is how it is done:

1. Make eye contact when someone talks to you. Don't look off into the distance, examine your shoes, or look over the speaker's head. Show your interest by focusing your attention on the person talking to you.
2. Use body language to show your interest in the speaker. Don't sit or stand stiffly with your arms crossed tightly over your chest, don't tap your foot or act impatient, and don't frown fiercely, roll your eyes, or otherwise act disinterested or disrespectful.
3. Try your best not to interrupt. When someone interrupts you, it makes you feel as though you didn't get a chance to finish your thoughts and that they aren't important to the other person.
4. Don't listen like a fence post. Nod your head or make an occasional encouraging comment, such as, "What happened next?" or, "Tell me more about that."

Body language tells us whether or not someone is open to a discussion. Putting up a hand as a stop signal or crossing arms over his or her chest are clues that a person is not open to listening.

Victims of bullying are often different in some way. Sometimes the source of bullying is jealousy. Other times it is insecurity and the bullies pick on others to feel better about themselves.

5. Give feedback to the speaker to be sure you understand, but feedback shouldn't be corny or foolish, such as, "Hmm, you don't say." Instead, try to get the person to say more. For example, if your friend says, "I hate English class," you might simply ask why. It could be your friend's underlying feeling is not that English class stinks but that her teacher isn't grading fairly or that someone in class is picking on her. The fact that you are genuinely listening can help, just as someone who actively listens to you can often help you avoid or resolve a conflict.[4]

As in anything else worth doing, active listening takes practice. Try practicing it the next time someone wants to talk to you, and you may find that what goes around comes around—because you have actively listened to someone else, they will truly listen to you.

One Type of Argument: Bullying

Bullying is a type of conflict that is often difficult to resolve because the victim wants it to stop, but the bullies feel powerful in controlling someone who is weaker or different from them. Bullies do not usually want to change the situation. Bullying involves calling people names, saying or writing nasty things about them, leaving them out of activities, not talking to them, threatening them, or making them feel scared, anxious, or embarrassed.

People bully for several reasons. Sometimes it makes them feel popular or important. Or they may feel jealous of or inferior to the people they bully, and they do it to even the score. Bullies also enjoy the sense of power and control they get when they pick on someone else. In some cases, bullies do not even realize that their behavior is hurtful, or they refuse to admit it. Whatever the reasons, bullying is wrong and creates serious external and internal conflicts for victims that should not go unnoticed or unresolved.

People who are victims of bullies are usually different from the group. They might be more attractive, smarter, shorter, taller, have nicer clothes, be of a different race, or simply seem too weak or frightened to fight back. Bullying is harmful because it makes victims feel bad about themselves and hate going to school, and sometimes it even makes them physically sick. Because bullying can cause depression, victims of bullying have even committed suicide. Suicide caused by bullying is called bullycide.[5]

Because bullying causes emotional and psychological harm and also often leads to physical harm, schools should not allow it to continue. Most victims of bullying cannot resolve the situation on their own and should ask for help from parents, teachers, counselors, or other trusted adults who have the power to intervene.

Bullying has become such a concern in schools that many school systems are dealing with it in special programs, assemblies, and counseling programs that emphasize how bullying is hurtful. According to the Bully Police USA, a national organization formed to speak for the victims of bullying and to lobby for state antibullying laws, as of March 2015, all fifty states have passed antibullying laws. The Bully Police USA website also reports that:

- Three out of every four students report that they have been bullied.
- Each month more than 250,000 students report that they have been physically attacked.
- Sixty-nine percent of students believe schools respond poorly to reports of bullying.
- Studies show that both bullies and victims have problems later in life because of bullying.[6]

One Student's Experience

Daryl endured peer abuse from very first year of school until the day that he graduated. He says of his experience: "I was bullied and teased constantly in school from kindergarten to the twelve grade. It wasn't easy to go through what I went through in regular school. Every year I was teased and bullied on a daily basis from Monday to Friday. I had to endure a lot in school from the name calling, physical abuse, and mental abuse. At times I felt like I was alone and that no one cared about me because of what I was going through."[7]

Miranda, who was bullied in elementary school, hoped to make a fresh start at a different school when she started sixth grade. Yet at her new school she was soon singled out for abuse: "There was this one boy who decided it was his mission to make my life there at school miserable. He tried to break my fingers in my locker when they were in the locker door by slamming the locker door shut on them. Thankfully I had pulled them out in time. He also would slam all my books to the ground, and once he tried to push me down a short flight of stairs in my school."

Individuals, such as Daryl and Miranda, who experience relentless abuse from their peers may begin to believe there is actually something wrong with them that invites bullying. They imagine they are somehow to blame for the abuse they suffer or that they had it coming. As Miranda says, "[They] started to make me wonder why I was getting bullied. I mean, was it something I was doing that was causing them to constantly tear me down? Was there something wrong with me?"[8]

Jordan Valacich, who was also severely bullied at school and became a teen spokesperson for the Bully Police, stresses that:

> No one is safe from bullying. If you are fat, skinny, ugly, pretty, smart, dumb, liked by the boys or not liked by the boys—there is no logic behind the bullying. You can't prepare yourself or do anything to keep it from happening to you except speak out and try to let people know about it and know that no one deserves this treatment, and we all have a right to go to school in peace. Don't just take it and do nothing; there are ways to stop it. Any adult at their work would sue for harassment over a lot less than many school kids are forced to go through on a daily basis. And they would win. But this is supposed to be a normal part of growing up for kids. If this is normal, I don't want to be![9]

Methods of Dealing With Bullies

Elizabeth Bennett is an expert on bullying, also known as peer abuse, who hosts Peerabuse.net, a website devoted to adult survivors of bullying. Bennett visits schools to speak about bullying and publishes a newsletter about peer abuse. She has the following suggestions for students, parents, and others for dealing with bullying:

- Document incidents of bullying. Save threatening e-mails, notes, and telephone messages left on answering machines. Keep a journal listing incidents, dates, and those involved. Whenever possible, use a video camera to record incidents in progress.
- Bullies don't want authorities to see them in action, so if it is happening to you or if you see it happening to someone else, tell adults in school, your parents, or law enforcement officers.
- When all else fails, your parents may want to contact an attorney because bullies violate your rights and often commit crimes, therefore they can sometimes be punished by court action.
- If you know others who are victims, form a support system. Get together to talk about your experiences and perhaps talk about possible solutions. Try not to be caught alone with bullies—travel to and from school with others if you can.
- Every state has an antibullying law. If you have documented incidents where you were the victim of bullies, you may have a legal case against your tormentors.[10]

Anyone can visit Bennett's website for help with a bullying problem, and she also provides links to other websites about bullying. Bennett also works with the Bully Police USA, and that website is another source of help.

Should You Fight Back?

Bullying can lead to fighting when the victim of abuse decides to fight back. Fighting can also result when parties in conflict let tempers

Bullying can take several forms. Sometimes it is anonymous; other times it's verbal. But on occasion it can involve physical violence. Physical fights are not a successful way to resolve conflict.

spiral out of control. The object of conflict resolution, obviously, is to solve problems before they reach this stage. Sometimes, however, a situation spins out of control so fast that violence erupts before anyone can stop it.

Ben, Clarice, Nancy, and Ted are middle school students who are using their study period to finish writing a skit due the next period for English class. As part of the assignment, they need to record the skit, and time is running short. When they go to sign out the tape recorder from the media center, Josh is using it and won't give it up. "I'm listening to a story," he tells Ben.

"That's not important now," Ben replies. "We need the tape recorder now."

"Too bad," Josh says, and Ben pushes him. Josh takes a swing at Ben, and soon the two boys are wrestling on the floor. The fight results in detention for both Ben and Josh, and Ben's group is unable to finish their English assignment on time.

Using force may seem like a good idea in the few seconds before tempers explode, but it seldom results in satisfactory problem solving. It takes patience to resolve conflicts peacefully, but results are generally helpful and lasting.

Skills for Resolving Conflicts

Resolving conflicts peacefully requires knowledge and skills that can be learned. In addition to creative listening, these skills include:

1. Communication: Talking to persons on the other side of the conflict without threatening or arguing.
2. Calm confrontation: Giving "I" messages to others. This involves telling others how you feel without accusing them. For example, instead of "You always put me down," say, "I feel put down when you . . ."
3. Controlling your behavior: Indicate that you are communicating respectfully by refraining from eye rolling,

shouting, name calling, or other threatening or disrespectful behavior.

4. Questioning: You can learn to ask pertinent questions to help pinpoint the concerns of the opposing side. For example, you might say, "You look angry. Are you?"
5. Being assertive without becoming aggressive: You can speak firmly in a negotiation without shouting, name calling, or using other aggressive behavior. "I will discuss the problem further, but I can't agree to all of your demands because . . ."
6. Providing helpful feedback: Clarifying the opposition's statements helps to clearly define the goals and expectations of the individuals involved so that misunderstandings do not continue to add fuel to the conflict. "You said that you want to resolve this quickly. Does that mean today, in a week, or do we have more time than that?"

These skills are worth learning because successfully resolving conflicts preserves relationships and gives you valuable negotiating skills that you can use for a lifetime. Knowing that you can successfully resolve conflicts also leads to a sense of pride and accomplishment that fosters self-esteem.

Even if you become skillful at resolving conflicts on your own, there may be situations where those skills do not work—as in bullying. In these cases, be sure to ask for help from an adult you trust. You can still be proud that you were resourceful enough to find a way to solve a problem.

4

Problems and Solutions

Being in conflict often brings out strong feelings in the opposing individuals or groups. When we experience conflict, our emotions can make it hard to imagine a possible resolution to the situation. Abby, a high school junior, wanted to attend college. Her grades were good in math and science, but she was far less interested in her speech and civics classes. Abby wanted to major in biology at a state university after high school graduation. Abby's father was a lawyer, however, and he was determined that Abby follow in his footsteps. Abby's mother, a paralegal, also wanted her to attend law school and told her often how wonderful it would be to have two attorneys in the family.

No matter how many times Abby tried to broach the subject of college, her parents were either too busy to listen or they lectured about the advantages of working as a lawyer. Abby had always been a quiet, dutiful daughter, and she could not bring herself to introduce the conflict she knew would follow when her parents learned of her intentions. Finally, Abby felt she could wait no longer, and she told her parents she was not going to attend law school. "I'm not even interested in law, and I know it would bore me to death," she said.

"I thought this had been decided," Abby's father said. "I don't want to hear any more nonsense about your not becoming a lawyer." He was clearly not listening to Abby and even threatened to withdraw financial support if she did not pursue a career in law.

Abby finally asked a trusted school counselor to mediate the dispute with her father. The counselor agreed and made an appointment to visit first with Abby's mother and father, then with Abby and her parents together. After reviewing her grades in science and math courses and her SAT scores, Abby's parents agreed that a course of study leading to a degree in biology might be the right choice for their daughter because she had a genuine interest in the field and a clear aptitude for science.

After several meetings with the school counselor, Abby's parents finally accepted the idea that their daughter would not become a lawyer. "As long as you get a college degree, we can live with your choice of major," Abby's parents told her.

Had Abby not told her parents how she felt, had the counselor not helped when she did tell her parents, or had her father stubbornly continued to refuse to hear Abby's argument, she might have enrolled in pre-law and been miserable. The odds were good, too, that Abby would not have succeeded in a field she felt forced to enter.

Abby and her parents were able to negotiate a solution to their conflict because several vital facts were present:

1. The relationship between Abby and her parents was important to all parties concerned.
2. Abby was concerned about her parents' interests.

3. Abby's parents were concerned about her interests, despite their attempt to force her to accept their plan.
4. Abby and her parents were striving for the same goals—that Abby should earn a college degree and be happy and successful in her chosen career.

For all of these reasons, Abby and her parents were eventually able to negotiate a solution. Abby took the first step toward negotiating a solution when she admitted to her parents that there was a problem.

Seeking a Solution

The goal for any negotiation is for everyone to win. While it is unlikely that both sides will get everything they want, for a negotiation to be successful, both sides must feel that they have won something. After two opposing sides have recognized that a conflict exists, according to Johnson and Johnson, the following six steps can help them successfully negotiate a solution:

1. **Describe what each person involved in the conflict wants.** If the two sides do not know what they want, there can be no basis for negotiation. This does not mean you simply demand that the other person change. And it is equally unhelpful for you to keep what you want to yourself, simply withdraw, and allow the other person to have whatever he or she wants from you.

Accurately defining your desires requires good communication skills. Use "I" statements, listen attentively, and paraphrase your opponent's statements to be sure you understand his or her exact meaning. For example: Judith's friend Grace has told everyone that Judith cheated on her boyfriend, Stan, and went out with Thom. The rumor is untrue. Stan is accusing Judith of cheating on him, Judith is angry with Grace, and the feud between the two girls has carried over into their classes. A teacher tells them to settle their differences or be sent to the principal's office, and the two girls arrange to meet in an empty classroom after school to talk. Grace is always late. Judith finally sees her coming, but Grace looks as though she has all the time in the world. Now Judith is really mad, and before she and Grace can sit down, she wants to start yelling at Grace. However, Judith remembers learning in a class that a person should use "I" statements instead of accusing someone when she is angry. So she tells Grace, "I want you to quit telling everybody that I cheated on Stan."

As part of step number one, the person on the other side should also describe what he or she wants. Grace replies, "Well, you told everyone I was jealous over you and Stan, and I was just getting even."

2. **Both parties should describe how they feel.** Before two sides can reach a solution, they need to understand why the problem exists, and this involves feelings. A problem would not exist if something had not triggered a strong emotion. If feelings are not brought into the open, chances are negotiation will be broken off before a solution can be found. Judith tells Grace she is angry and hurt that someone she considered a friend would go behind her back and talk about her. Grace tells Judith that she, too, was angry and hurt when Judith told others that Grace was jealous.

3. **Exchange reasons for positions.** Judith tells Grace she thought she was jealous because Grace did not invite her to her birthday slumber party. Grace answered that she didn't ask Judith because she heard she wouldn't come if she did ask her.

4. **Understand each other's point of view.** More conversation should follow between Judith and Gracc until each can see why the other behaved as she did. They don't have to agree with the behavior—just try to see why it occurred.

5. **Create options that will benefit both parties.** The two girls can suggest options to each other that might include ending the friendship, agreeing to always ask each other to birthday events, and agreeing not to spread rumors about each other.

When you have a job, you need to negotiate interactions with other people from the moment you're hired. You may also need to know how to use negotiation to resolve conflicts with your employer or other employees.

6. **Reach a wise agreement.**[1] A wise agreement will take into consideration the wants and feelings of both parties and will not make one party the winner and the other the loser. It will allow both sides to win something and should not be a temporary stopgap but a long-term solution to the problem.

Reaching an agreement through negotiation is not always as easy as it sounds. Negotiations often get stuck because one or both parties don't want to give up something of value. The human resources department at the University of Wisconsin in Madison suggests the following ten strategies to consider when negotiations get stuck.

1. When stuck, talk about how you feel for a while. You can always get back to the original issue.
2. Try reframing the issue. That is, use different words to describe your view of the conflict.
3. If the conflict seems overwhelming because so many different issues have been brought up, break it into smaller bites. This can help you get back to the basic reasons for the conflict.
4. Clarify, clarify, clarify. Keep restating what you think the other person is saying so it is obvious you are making an effort to understand. This can move the other side to respond positively to your efforts.
5. Stay flexible. One or both sides may be trapped by their thinking. Come up with new options for solving the problem to get everyone out of the rut that is stalling negotiations.
6. Emphasize those areas where you agree. It could be that you have been focusing only on your disagreements, and coming up with areas of agreement may be just what is needed to move negotiations forward.

7. Clarify the guidelines you are using to evaluate the conflict. For example, if you have based the discussion solely on comments that started the conflict ("He called me a liar"), try moving on to feelings that have kept the conflict going and what can be done about them.
8. Return to your ground rules. Rules for negotiation may have been lost as the discussion went on. Are you raising your voice now when you weren't before? Is your opponent resorting to name calling when you both agreed this was not acceptable behavior? Go over the rules again and make sure both sides are following them.
9. Take a break. Agree to stop the discussion for an hour or a day, for example, while you think of new options for a solution or simply let your emotions wind down.
10. Before you walk away, go over all possible solutions again. Most likely you will reach some sort of agreement, but if the negotiation is still deadlocked, you may have to walk away.[2]

Here are additional tips to help you negotiate solutions to conflicts:

- Don't wait too long to tell the other side your concerns. If you stew and become angry and resentful, when you finally confront the other person you will likely vent your anger instead of calmly stating what you want.
- Don't let emotions rule. Remind yourself to remain calm even if others are not.
- Never negotiate to win if it means the other side must lose. This breeds anger and resentment and is not a true resolution to conflict. A win-win solution works best.
- Keep an open mind. As you listen to others, perhaps you will begin to see their side so you can negotiate a solution that leaves everyone satisfied.

- Use your sense of humor, but don't laugh at the other person if he or she seems angry or sad. Don't make fun of the other person's wants, needs, or suggested solutions. If you can laugh at yourself, however, share the joke with others involved in the conflict resolution.
- If you have some sort of solution in mind as you begin negotiating, share it. If it works, you have saved time. If the other person doesn't like it, you have lost nothing.
- Stay flexible so you can keep offering suggestions for a solution even though you don't like some of the suggested options.
- Ask open-ended questions when you are trying to understand the other's position. An answer that explains is more revealing than a yes or no.
- Don't let the discussion get off track. When it seems to have degenerated into extended arguing, stop and continue another day.
- Decide what you want as opposed to what you need. If you are negotiating with your employer for more pay, for instance, you may want twice what you are getting, health benefits, and a four-week paid vacation. If you know you can't possibly get all you want, decide what you need—perhaps to work more hours would satisfy your financial needs—and negotiate for that.
- If it becomes clear that a resolution can never be reached, you and your opponent may have to simply agree to disagree and go your separate ways.

Conflicting Values

Sometimes conflicts go beyond relationships with others in your school or home. Sometimes you see something happening in the wider world that conflicts with your values so much that you feel compelled to take action. For instance, maybe you feel so strongly about child labor that you refuse to buy any products made by companies that employ children overseas. Or maybe you are so against killing animals for their fur or as food you boycott fashions that use real animal fur and become a vegetarian. There is no relationship to preserve here, but your feelings and opinions are so strong that you want things to change. In cases where your goal is change on a large scale, such nonviolent activities as marches, sit-ins, and boycotts of products are possible ways to show your concern.

Student Diplomacy

When ordinary people take peaceful, thoughtful stands against injustice, social change is often the result. And these ordinary people are not always adults. Tommy McManus, a former president of Project RACE Teens, didn't think it was right for students to check only one box for race on school forms. He convinced the dean of admissions at his New Jersey high school to change the application form to allow multiracial students to identify all parts of their heritage. Tommy proposed that the wording on forms be changed to read, "If you are multiracial, you may select two or more boxes." Project RACE activists want this option on all forms, including school enrollment, school tests, medical forms, hospital admissions, clinical trials, and government documents.[3]

Students at Pelican Island Elementary in Florida became worried about the fate of the scrub jay, an endangered species in their area. The bird's habitat was rapidly being replaced by housing developments. The students formed an Eco-Troop and made dozens of presentations to the school board, the Indian River County Commission, their US Representative, and the US Secretary of the Interior Department. They showed why the scrub jay's habitat should be protected. Eventually, they received a matching $200,000 grant from the US Fish and Wildlife Service to purchase undeveloped lots to create a wildlife sanctuary.[4]

Young people have also brought about change in places far beyond their own communities. In 2009, an eleven-year-old Pakistani schoolgirl named Malala Yousafzai began writing a blog about her experiences. The valley in western Pakistan where she lived

Malala Yousafzai was awarded the prestigious Nobel Peace Prize for raising awareness and enacting change. The eighteen-year-old was honored for speaking out against the Taliban's mistreatment of women.

had come under control of the Taliban, an organization of Muslim fundamentalists who believe that girls and women should not have the same rights as men. They think it is a crime for females to attend school or even to go shopping. Girls and women who break these rules are severely punished and sometimes killed. Malala had to write her blog under a pen name to protect herself from retaliation. Taliban militants had been systematically destroying girls' schools in the region where Malala lived. She wrote that she was worried the same thing would happen to her school. Many people read her blog and shared it with others.

Before long, Malala's identity became known. The Taliban targeted Malala and her family, and the Yousafzais knew that their lives were in danger. Despite the risk, Malala became even more outspoken about the rights of girls to have an education. In 2009, a documentary was made about her. In 2012, the Pakistani government awarded her the National Peace Award, which today is called the Malala Peace Prize, for individuals under eighteen.

In October of 2012, Taliban militants boarded Malala's school bus in northwest Pakistan. A gunman asked for her name, then aimed his pistol at her and fired three times. Malala was shot in the head, and two of her school friends were wounded in the attack. She was taken to a military hospital, where she underwent a five-hour operation to remove the bullet that had passed through her skull. Eventually she was flown to the United Kingdom for additional operations.

In the days after the shootings, people all around the world expressed outrage at the attempt on Malala's life. In Pakistan, more than two million people signed a Right to Education petition, which led to a bill being passed in Pakistan that, for the first time, established the right to education as a law.[5]

Over time, Malala recovered from the shooting. She refused to be silenced and continued to speak out in support of girls' rights to education. Media coverage helped Malala's cause to mushroom into an international movement. In 2014, Malala was awarded the Nobel

Peace Prize. At age seventeen, she was the youngest ever recipient of the award.

Famous Peacemakers

Leaders who advocate for social change are often people who have become skillful at conflict resolution. Two such leaders in the twentieth century were Mahatma Mohandas K. Gandhi (Mahatma is a title that means "Great Soul") and Archbishop Desmond Tutu. Mohandas Gandhi was born in Porbandar, India, on October 2, 1869, to parents of the merchant class. In 1891, he received a law degree from University College in London. He was admitted to the British bar in 1891 at the age of twenty-two. Gandhi returned to India to practice law but was largely unsuccessful until an Indian firm with interests in South Africa hired him to represent them. Upon arriving in South Africa, Gandhi found that he was treated as inferior because of his race. On trains, for example, even though he had purchased a first-class ticket, he was only allowed to ride in the third-class coach. When he refused, the police forced him off the train. Furthermore, because he was Indian, he could not vote without paying a poll tax, obtaining a business license, or owning land, and the South African government did not recognize marriages between Indian couples as legal.

Gandhi spent twenty years in South Africa, where he practiced passive resistance against uncooperative South African authorities and encouraged other Indians to follow him. He knew that it was important to maintain a relationship with government authorities in order to encourage negotiation. But he also realized that he had to make the authorities aware of unfair practices and the people's objection to them before the people could hope for change. He did this peacefully, such as when he refused to register and be fingerprinted—a requirement that applied only to Indian immigrants in South Africa.

Gandhi was arrested and imprisoned many times for his nonviolent civil disobedience, and sometimes his wife was also

Mahatma Gandhi used nonviolent civil disobedience to lead India to independence from Great Britain. Gandhi's methods of conflict resolution were later used by civil rights leader Martin Luther King Jr.

arrested and jailed for her husband's acts. In 1896, Gandhi was attacked and beaten by angry whites, but he continued his campaign against racism. He had so many followers that in 1914 the Union of South Africa made some concessions—Indian marriages would be legally recognized, and Indians could vote without being charged a poll tax.

Great Britain ruled India, and in 1914, when Gandhi and his family returned, he and his followers campaigned for India to become independent from British rule. His nonviolent protest was known as *satyagraha*, which means "truth force"—a combination of the Hindu words for truth and holding firmly. His followers grew until they became a hindrance to business by squatting in the streets and government buildings while they demonstrated for independence from Great Britain. Britain passed the Rowlatt Acts in 1920, which gave the government greater emergency powers to deal with revolutionary acts, including nonviolent opposition. Gandhi and his followers again used passive resistance to demonstrate against the Rowlatt Acts. Frustrated British soldiers shot and killed many of the protestors. Gandhi stepped up his campaign and was arrested but quickly released.

Gandhi and his followers then effectively boycotted British goods. Gandhi hoped to see cottage industries, such as spinning, revived in India to help resolve poverty among the lower classes. He became an international symbol for a free India and passive resistance. His habits of fasting, prayer, and meditation were well known by admirers. He was also known for his generous treatment of people of all races and creeds. "An eye for an eye," he once said, "only ends up making the whole world blind."[6]

In 1921 the Indian National Congress, an influential organization for Indian independence, gave Gandhi complete executive authority. Soon after, armed revolts against the British government increased. Gandhi was dismayed that people on both sides were killed, and he declared his civil disobedience movement a failure and ended it for the time being.

In 1930, Gandhi resumed civil disobedience when he began an antigovernment campaign against taxes—in particular, the salt tax. In a march that lasted twenty-four days, he led thousands of followers to the Arabian Sea, where they made salt by evaporating seawater. This was illegal, and Gandhi and sixty thousand others were arrested. Gandhi was released from prison in 1931.

Again and again Gandhi practiced passive resistance against British rule. He was jailed many times, but he never wavered from his goal of Indian independence. He fasted many times to protest violence. Finally, in 1947, partly to appease Gandhi and his many followers, the British government granted Indian independence. Because of religious divisions, two separate states were created—India, which was mainly Hindu, and Pakistan, which was mainly Muslim. Gandhi did not want his country divided, but he finally gave in and hoped that two separate states might bring peace between the Muslims and Hindus. A Hindu fanatic named Nathuram Godse assassinated Mohandas Gandhi in 1948. History has remembered Gandhi as an international symbol of nonviolent resistance to racism and injustice.

Archbishop Desmond Tutu is another person famous for encouraging nonviolent protest against the government in power as a means of social change. He was born in Klerksdorp, South Africa, in 1931. His father was a teacher, and his mother was a domestic worker. Tutu was raised by sympathetic and tolerant parents, and he later said of his upbringing, "I never learnt to hate."[7]

While Desmond Tutu was growing up in South Africa, he lived under apartheid—a strict policy of racial segregation ordered by the all-white National Party government. Under the apartheid system, all South Africans were assigned to one of the following races: white, African, Asian, or colored. Workers from India were classified as Asian. Signs were erected throughout the country designating segregated areas. All races had separate housing, separate public toilets, and separate parks and beaches. Black workers could not form unions, had no representation in the government, and like

Bishop Desmond Tutu encouraged peaceful protest to end apartheid, a system of legalized racial segregation, in his native South Africa.

other nonwhite races, were paid much lower wages than white workers. Mixed marriages were against the law, travel was forbidden without a government-issued pass, and jobs could be categorized as white-only. Nonwhite races had separate schools that were inferior to white schools, and separate universities and colleges were also established.

During the years when apartheid was enforced in South Africa, there were many laws that discriminated against nonwhite South Africans. For example, the Suppression of Communism Act of 1950 let the government classify anyone who objected to apartheid as a communist, and that person was then subject to being banned from public meetings and holding public office and was under indefinite house arrest. The Native Administration Act of 1956 allowed the government to banish native Africans to remote areas of the country.

Despite strict segregation laws, in 1953 Desmond Tutu earned a teaching degree from Pretoria Bantu Normal College in Johannesburg, South Africa. He had wanted to become a doctor, but his parents could not afford to send him to medical school. He taught school in South Africa for three years but was discouraged by the poor schools for black students in his country. He decided to become an Anglican priest, resigned from teaching, and began his theological training in 1958.

Tutu was in Great Britain furthering his theological education while the antiapartheid movement was gaining momentum in South Africa. After an incident in 1960 in which sixty-nine peaceful protesters were killed by police and following the establishment of harsher laws discriminating against nonwhites, the African National Congress (ANC) abandoned peaceful protest against apartheid. The ANC, led by Nelson Mandela, formed an armed unit and battled government forces military style. As a result, in 1968, Mandela and seven other black ANC leaders were arrested for trying to violently overthrow the government. They received life sentences in prison.

By 1972 Desmond Tutu had finished his theology education and was in London serving as an assistant director of the World Council of Churches. He returned to South Africa in 1975 and was appointed dean of St. Mary's Cathedral in Johannesburg. He was the first black to hold that position. By this time, the United Nations had declared apartheid "a crime against humanity,"[8] and Tutu was gaining world attention as a spokesperson for the antiapartheid movement.

In 1978 Tutu was appointed the first black general secretary of the South African Council of Churches. He encouraged black people to use peaceful resistance to protest apartheid, and he urged the world community to stop trading with South Africa until apartheid was repealed. In response, the government canceled his passport.

Ten years later, in 1988, by government order, the headquarters of the South African Council of Churches was bombed. Twenty-one people were injured.

Tutu became a spokesperson for the United Democratic Front, an organization with a membership of three million that was formed to protest apartheid. In 1984, Tutu received the Nobel Peace Prize, which is awarded yearly to individuals who make major contributions to world peace. The Nobel Committee recognized Tutu for "the courage and heroism shown by black South Africans in their use of peaceful methods in the struggle against apartheid."[9] Tutu became a bishop in 1985 and an archbishop in 1986.

By 1990, economic sanctions against South Africa had begun to have an effect, and the government was beginning to see that it would have to relax apartheid rules. As part of this softer stance, Nelson Mandela was released from prison. In 1994, the all-race ANC was elected to power, and the National Party became the minority party in South African government. A new South African constitution took effect in 1996 that contained a bill of rights and ended discrimination against all minorities, including whites.

Throughout the years of apartheid, Tutu's voice was heard worldwide condemning segregation and urging peaceful resistance to its many restrictions. Today Desmond Tutu has retired as archbishop and runs the Tutu Peace Center in Cape Town, South Africa. In 2007, he joined The Elders, a group of world leaders that includes former Secretary-General of the United Nations Kofi Annan and former President Jimmy Carter. They meet to discuss ways to promote human rights and world peace.

Mohandas Gandhi and Archbishop Desmond Tutu put themselves in personal danger in their attempts to right society's wrongs through nonviolent opposition. No matter how often they or their followers were physically attacked, they stayed their course and practiced passive resistance in the face of racism. Most of us will never be called upon to face such opposition as we resolve conflicts in our lives. We can, however, remember their legacy of nonviolence as we deal with individuals and groups whose values and behavior are so different from our own that it seems we can never reconcile. Those are the situations where the conflict resolution techniques described in this chapter can come to our aid. "It is the acid test of nonviolence," Gandhi once said, "that in a nonviolent conflict there is no rancor left behind and, in the end, the enemies are converted into friends."[10]

5

How Peer Mediation Works

Peer mediation is a program used in schools throughout the United States. This form of conflict resolution relies on negotiation and mediation, where students are trained to mediate conflicts between their peers. Mediation implies the involvement of a nonjudgmental, objective person who helps the two opposing parties involved in a dispute settle their differences, usually when other methods have failed.

Consider the following scenario: Craig, a high school junior, had a party one weekend while his parents were out of town. Carlene, a sophomore, crashed the party. Carlene's boyfriend, Josh, was there with another girl, Gloria. Carlene confronted Josh and told him she never wanted to see him again. She pushed him, which made Josh angry. Josh could not hit Carlene, so he punched David, who had been trying to get the shouting couple to step outside to settle their differences. When Josh hit David, David's friend, Barry, hit Josh.

Soon the party guests were taking sides in the melee, and a nervous Craig called the police. David had been hit so hard he was taken to the hospital emergency room. The police called Craig's parents at their out-of-town hotel, and they started home.

As the result of the party-turned-brawl, Craig was grounded for a month with no television, computer, or telephone privileges. Josh faced an assault charge since David's injuries had led to an overnight stay in the hospital. Several of the boys and girls who had attended the party were still arguing at school several days later.

The above scenario is an example of an interpersonal conflict (Carlene's confrontation with Josh) that mushroomed into an intergroup conflict. Since the disgruntled parties continued to disagree and were disrupting their respective classes at school, it is also an example of a conflict that might be resolved through peer mediation.

Goals of Peer Mediation

Peer mediation programs let students within the same age group help resolve disputes between two people or small groups. In some cases, peer mediation programs may also help solve low-level discipline problems in schools. For example, students who swear at other students or start fights may be allowed to agree to peer mediation instead of being sent to the principal's office. In some schools, peer mediation is used in addition to other disciplinary measures. Mediation is voluntary for everyone involved unless it is offered as a choice instead of disciplinary action. Peer mediators do not make decisions to end disputes. They help the two sides in a conflict reach an agreement to avoid further trouble.

There are several reasons why peer mediation is useful, including the following:

1. It can help prevent fights, which often end in suspension from school.

2. It provides a forum for students, parents, teachers, and school administrators to talk when necessary.
3. It can keep hurt feelings from resulting in the loss of friends.
4. It encourages students of all ages to solve problems on their own when possible without help from adults.
5. It helps students learn to live peacefully with people who are different from them.

How Peer Mediation Works

Peer mediation processes vary with the schools that use them, but most programs incorporate the following features:

1. Two or more students refer themselves or are referred by teachers, counselors, or school administrators to a school's peer mediation program.
2. One or two trained student mediators are chosen to help end the dispute. In many schools, mediators work in pairs.
3. The mediator introduces himself or herself to those involved in the conflict, and the parties agree on the ground rules. In some programs, the disputants, or those involved in a dispute, fill out pre-session forms establishing the rules.

Rules generally include:

- Participants must tell the truth and listen respectfully without interrupting.
- Participants should be committed to solving the problem.
- No shouting, name calling, or other aggressive responses.
- Everything discussed in sessions is kept confidential unless a danger is revealed.
- Both sides must try to calmly explain the problem.

- Both sides must agree on a solution if a plausible one is suggested.
- The parties must take responsibility for carrying out the agreement.

4. Each party is asked to describe the problem. The mediator listens to each party and writes down an agreed upon agenda that includes all the elements of the dispute.
5. Each party in the dispute tells his or her side of the story to each other. The goal is to bring out all the facts and feelings surrounding the dispute. The mediator asks questions so the disputants can see the problem from different perspectives.
6. The mediator asks both parties to brainstorm suggestions for solving the problem. The mediator writes down all the possible solutions and indicates those that were mutually agreed upon. If no solutions are suggested, participants return to earlier steps. Sometimes additional sessions are required, or the mediator may want to meet with the parties separately.
7. The mediator writes a contract using the agreed upon solutions, and everyone signs it.
8. A follow-up session date is set so the two parties can tell how the solution is working.[1]

Peer Mediation in Action

In the previous scenario, which is based on a real-life situation, a fight broke out at a party. Since emotions spilled over to the classroom, the off-campus fight became a source of disruption at school. Carlene had conducted a gossip campaign against Gloria, and Gloria had retaliated by spreading the rumor that Carlene had stolen a friend's purse. "I don't like what you've been saying about me," Carlene told Gloria in the hallway between classes. "Stop it or you'll be sorry."

"I don't know what you're talking about," Gloria responded. "And you're a fine one to talk—all the lies you've been spreading about me."

When the two girls continued their whispering campaigns against each other in math class, their teacher, Mr. Thomas, was annoyed. He was tired of the disruption and asked the girls to stay after class. "It's apparent the two of you aren't getting along," he said. "This isn't the first time you have disrupted class. I can send you to the office, or you can request a peer mediation session." Since neither girl wanted to face the principal, both Carlene and Gloria agreed to peer mediation.

Marsha, the peer mediator chosen to help Carlene and Gloria, was not sure she could help the girls because the conflict had simmered for so long that both girls were extremely hostile. At the beginning of the mediation process, it did seem as though finding a mutually agreeable solution would be impossible. Each girl blamed the other for the conflict. "If you hadn't stolen my boyfriend, none of this would have happened," Carlene accused.

"I didn't know he was your boyfriend when he asked me out," Gloria replied. "And you can have him, anyway. I didn't like him that well."

"And I resent your calling me a thief," Carlene countered. "I've never stolen anything in my life."

As she worked through the mediation process, Marsha found that there were many areas where common ground might be found. Carlene had been about to break up with Josh even before the ill-fated party because they were not getting along well. His date with Gloria gave her the excuse she needed to break off the relationship. Marsha began to realize that Carlene was actually most jealous of Gloria because of her popularity and the fact that she would undoubtedly be elected to the cheerleading squad—a dream that Carlene was too insecure to pursue. Gloria was finally able to admit that she had made up the story about Carlene stealing and that

Carlene's whispering campaign against her was more annoying than damaging.

The solution both girls accepted was that they would each stop spreading malicious rumors about each other and would work on controlling their respective tempers. A session was scheduled for the following month to assess how well the solution was working. The girls would probably never become close friends or move within the same friendship circles, but if they stopped gossiping about each other, the mediation process would have been successful.

Just as a person must constantly practice to become a good athlete, musician, artist, or public speaker, he or she must practice constantly to become a skilled mediator. Often even student mediators are surprised at how well the process can work. "It's amazing," Ruth Perlstein and Gloria Thrall report in their book, *Conflict Resolution Activities for Secondary Students*. "They [the disputants] seemed to be getting nowhere and we kept asking them what the problem really is and all of a sudden a light bulb went on . . . they came in ready to kill each other and walked out smiling."[2]

Here is a step-by-step breakdown of the mediation process Marsha conducted.

1. Marsha began by introducing herself to Carlene and Gloria. "My name is Marsha, and I'm here to help you resolve your conflict. I won't take sides, and I don't make decisions for you. I can't make you do anything, but I'll help you decide for yourselves how to resolve your conflict."
2. Marsha then asked the two disputants if they would agree:
    - To try to identify the problem
    - To try to solve the problem
    - Not to interrupt each other
    - Not to call each other names or put each other down
    - To tell the truth

Peer mediation can be effective in resolving conflicts. The mediator does not take sides, and he or she asks both parties to brainstorm ideas for resolution.

- To keep everything discussed in the mediation session confidential

3. Carlene and Gloria agreed to follow the session rules.
4. Marsha asked each disputant to give her version of the problem.
5. Marsha asked Carlene and Gloria to brainstorm possible solutions to the problem. Brainstorming means to suggest ideas as fast as you think of them without worrying if they sound stupid or unworkable. The idea is to quickly get as many suggestions as possible and sort them out later.
6. To help the disputants arrive at the best solution, Marsha asked them to discuss the consequences of each solution.
7. Marsha asked Carlene and Gloria which solution each preferred.
8. The two disputants were asked if they thought they could keep their side of the agreement.
9. The agreement was written out, and Marsha, Carlene, and Gloria signed it.
10. Marsha asked Carlene and Gloria to come back in one month to discuss how the chosen solution was working.

Training in Peer Mediation

In some school peer mediation programs, the entire student body receives training in conflict resolution and peer mediation, and any student may be considered as a possible peer mediator. In other programs, students volunteer to receive mediation training, and those most qualified are accepted. The panel of adults that chooses students to participate in the peer mediation program may consist of a counselor, a teacher, an administrator, or other school personnel. Students who participate in a peer mediation program should reflect the school's diversity, including cultures, gender, behavior, academic performance, social status, and race. Some schools claim that those students who have been labeled troublesome often make the best mediators.

Students should be informed of the selection procedure, and recommendations and referrals should be considered when choosing students to train as mediators. When students choose to train as mediators, they are committing to continued skills development, willingness to conduct sessions as a team, and to mentor new trainees.

Students and adults who are chosen to be peer mediators must receive training in conflict resolution skills. Peer mediation training usually includes role-playing, where students take the part of someone involved in a conflict and act accordingly. Most training sessions also give students a variety of problems to discuss. They try to decide what caused the problem, how the problem got out of hand, and how it might be solved. Training may also include sitting in with an experienced mediator to see how a mediation session is conducted. Training may consist of a semester-long class in conflict resolution and mediation or of workshops of varying duration.

Students who have participated in peer mediation sessions or programs agree that those who make the best mediators are:

- Trustworthy
- Good listeners
- Fair and do not take sides
- Able to maintain confidentiality

They are not:

- Someone who gives orders or advice
- Judgmental
- Individuals who talk about other students' conflicts
- Individuals who interrupt or focus attention on themselves

Some schools have a group of peer mediators who are trained specifically to resolve conflicts. The training they undergo is intense and can include role-playing scenarios.

Problems Peer Mediators Handle

School peer mediation programs have reported that student mediators can best handle the following types of problems: rumor and gossip, relationship difficulties, harassment, racial and cultural confrontations, classroom or extracurricular disputes, minor assaults and fighting, cheating, and vandalism. Student mediators do not handle cases that involve sexual abuse, criminal assault, theft, suicide, drug use, weapon possession, or those that involve legal problems, such as one party wanting to sue another. These types of problems require professional help from counselors, police officers, physicians, or attorneys.

The Benefits of Peer Mediation

According to peer mediation experts, research shows that students who receive conflict resolution training learn tolerance, kindness, and nonviolence, and they learn to restore relationships rather than destroy them through retribution. The positive results for schools include:

- A safer, more caring school environment
- Less classroom time spent on discipline and more time for teaching and learning
- Fewer disciplinary problems referred to the office
- Reduced suspensions, detentions, and expulsions
- A reduction in violence, vandalism, and chronic school absenteeism

Teachers, school administrators, and parents have observed the following benefits for students who participate in peer mediation sessions or are trained to be peer mediators:

- Improved communications among students, teachers, administrators, and parents
- Gaining a direct forum for resolving conflicts that does not require administrative attention or punitive disciplinary action
- An increased sense of competence, responsibility, and accountability
- Improved academic performance
- Enhanced social and coping skills

Students say peer mediation programs have helped them improve the following skills:

- Listening
- Communication
- Anger management and emotional self-awareness

In some situations, it is best to work with a mediator who is not a peer. A fair, trusted adult who can hear out both sides and put the conflict in perspective can help both sides come to an agreement.

- Critical thinking
- Problem solving
- Taking responsibility and being accountable
- Assertiveness
- Team or group collaboration
- Leadership

Sometimes despite efforts of peer mediators and disputants involved in a conflict, one or more individuals are so difficult to deal with that a conflict seems impossible to resolve. The following chapter shows how to avoid conflict or keep conflict resolution on track when certain individuals are behaving at their worst.

6

Difficult Personality Types

Oprah Winfrey once advised, "Surround yourself only with people who are going to lift you higher." That is not always possible, however, because the world is full of difficult people. You encounter them all the time. Your teacher may pair you up with a lab partner who whines about the work and distracts you during class. Your manager at the supermarket fails to explain tasks clearly and then insults you when you make a mistake. Do the following types of people sound familiar?

"Sure, I'll help," Ray promised when asked to bring his pickup to help collect materials from various downtown merchants to decorate for the prom. As usual, Ray didn't show up, which left the prom decorating committee without enough help.

"Let's just get this done so we can get out of here," Susan, a member of the prom decorating committee, remarked as she began throwing streamers up any old way. Typically, someone else had to come along behind Susan and correct her work.

"No, I won't help this year," Joe said when asked to help decorate for the prom. "I worked harder than anyone last year, and no one even appreciated it. I heard some kids actually criticizing the decorating theme we chose. That's the way it always goes. You work, work, work, and you're never appreciated—lucky if you even get a thank you."

Carla agreed to work on the decorating committee but criticized everyone else's work. "You can decorate that way if you want," she offered, "but I'm telling you it won't work. That tape won't hold up the streamers, and everything will fall down on the dancers. But go ahead. Even though I know what I'm talking about, don't take my advice."

"You have a terrible sense of color coordination," Mel told Stephen. "You must be one of those guys who is red-green color-blind. That combination of streamers you've chosen looks sick."

"I might help later," Richard told Janice, the chair of the prom decorating committee, "if I can get my homework done." It was typical of Richard to say maybe when asked to contribute to a project, so Janice didn't count on him to show up.

Are there individuals like these in your life? Do they drive you to distraction when you have to work with them? Or (gasp) are you one of those people that other people dislike and avoid?

Some people change their behavior as the situation warrants. They may be happy-go-lucky and easy to get along with as long as nothing is asked of them. Or they may have certain dislikes that, if mentioned, will set them off on a tirade. Others may be so obsessed with doing a job perfectly that they never get the job done at all.

Dealing With Difficult People

"I can't stand him," is a common statement. We may not know why, exactly, we can't stand someone. We just know that some people just rub us the wrong way, and we would rather not be around them.

But what if you have to work with that person on a school project or other assignment, as in the previous example? Then it would probably help your relationships and your peace of mind if you knew how to bring out the best in these people, or at least to tolerate them until the job is finished.

In *Dealing With People You Can't Stand: How to Bring Out the Best in People at Their Worst,* physicians Rick Brinkman and Rick Kirschner explain that most people are either task-oriented or people-oriented. Task-oriented individuals want to:

- Get the job done on time
- Get the job done right

People-oriented individuals are more concerned with:

- Having people like them as they work on a project
- Impressing their coworkers with their knowledge and expertise

When any of these four goals are thwarted, Brinkman and Kirschner assert, people can respond in ways that make others upset or wary.[1] Several of the most common irritating personality types are portrayed in the decorating committee example.

1. Ray is a yes person. He says yes to everyone who asks him to do something and hopes to make people like him. On the same day he promised to use his pickup to haul prom decorations, he had also promised his mother to haul used furniture to the auction barn, the football coach to haul sports equipment, and his neighbor to haul gardening tools. Typical of most yes people, Ray failed to keep any of his commitments. Therefore, instead of making everyone happy as he intended, he angered everyone who had expected him to help.

2. Susan's goal was simply to get the decorating task done so she could go on to something she would rather do. She lost sight of doing the task well in her haste to finish the job. Others were angry that they had to spend time fixing every decoration Susan hastily put up.
3. Joe's mantra is "no one appreciates me." Others are so accustomed to hearing Joe's lament that they turn a deaf ear to his complaints. Those who had worked with Joe before were actually relieved that he said no to serving on the decorating committee.
4. Carla is a no person. She is also a know-it-all who believes she is the only person who knows how to do a job correctly. She was willing to serve on the prom decoration committee, but she made everyone so miserable with her constant criticizing and lecturing that they wished she had declined.
5. Mel will protest to Stephen that he was only kidding if Stephen gets angry over his remarks, but Mel actually seems to enjoy putting others down. His not-so-subtle personal barbs make him feel superior to others and make others feel self-conscious, put down, and angry.
6. Richard believes he has found the answer to always pleasing others. If he says maybe to every request for his time or services, he has not actually turned anyone down, and everyone should like him. What he has failed to realize is that when he says maybe then does not show up, he has taught others to distrust and possibly even to dislike him.

Other problem people can include:

- Jokers who handle every conflict by making jokes about the problem instead of discussing it seriously

One type of difficult person is the know-it-all. These people think they know best and rarely give others the chance to speak up or make suggestions. Conflicts with know-it-alls are often one-sided.

- Blockers who shoot down any ideas for resolving a conflict that didn't come from them
- Hagglers who seem to want to keep the conflict alive by constantly wrangling and arguing
- Deceitful, underhanded individuals who act as though they want to resolve a conflict but sabotage any attempt to reach agreement.

These examples represent just a few of the annoying people you encounter in your daily life. The people described above are annoying but not particularly toxic. Dealing with the yes person, the maybe person, the know-it-all, the naysayer, the joker, and the critical person can be time-consuming and exasperating, but there are ways to respond to these people that can keep you from facing a conflict every time you associate with them:

1. Choose face-to-face talks over communicating through a third person. For example, instead of having your friend Kevin tell Annie that you're angry with her, tell Annie yourself what is bothering you. There is no need to put friends in the middle of a disagreement when you can handle it yourself just as well.
2. Put the person in proper perspective. Try not to take his or her behavior personally because a difficult person deals with everyone in the same manner. Be straightforward and unemotional, and be gracious and courteous even when the other person is rude. For example, you know Donna criticizes everyone, but when she tells you your skirt and blouse don't match, your first impulse is to snap, "Who made you the fashion police?" Then Donna snaps back, and the two of you are angry. Instead of snapping at Donna, which would probably be everyone's first impulse, try saying something such as, "Thanks, Donna. That's good to know." Keep your tone pleasant and walk away. Forget Donna's remark and

go about your day. Donna's probably feeling disappointed that she did not get to you, and you can smile knowing you avoided a conflict and cut Donna off at the pass.

3. Listen patiently to the know-it-alls, naysayers, and critical people, then indicate that you have heard them and will consider their comments. Emphasize positive points and do not dwell on the negative.

4. Learn to respond to difficult people by asking questions instead of making accusations. Give and request frequent feedback. Tell the person the truth from your viewpoint: "Ray, you've said yes before and failed to follow through. We really need your help this time, so we'll be counting on you." For the yes person and the maybe person, follow up your face-to-face conversation with a telephone reminder that you need their help on the designated time and date.

   For know-it-alls, naysayers, and critical people, you can be direct without playing their game. "I'm surprised that you think this won't work because we have done it this way several times and it's always worked before." "We've heard your criticism, Carl. What is your suggestion for doing it a better way?" And so on. These three personality types want most of all to be noticed, and if you acknowledge their complaints and criticisms, they may eventually cooperate.

5. Don't base your goals on expecting the difficult person to change.

Toxic Personality Types

According to Mike Moore, an international speaker and writer on human potential and motivation, toxic refers to those people who are openly or stealthily abusive and can affect you in one or more of the following ways:

- Rob you of your dignity

Communicating with difficult personality types can be challenging. You will be successful if you remain calm, listen patiently, and keep an open mind. Interrupting the difficult personality type or rolling your eyes at him or her will not yield successful results.

- Destroy your self-confidence or self-esteem
- Increase your stress levels
- Destroy your morale
- Make you think negative thoughts
- Decrease your productivity
- Simply make your life miserable[2]

The toxic people you are most likely to have to deal with include bulldozers, volcanoes, and snipers. These types of people may also turn into one of the bullies discussed earlier in this resource, and bullies are usually a more serious problem than the aggressive personalities discussed below.

1. **Bulldozers** are intimidating. When they approach a group or enter a room, everyone wants to dive for cover. Their only goal is to get their own way, and they do not care whom they have to push aside or travel over to get it. Their aggressive behavior is meant to defuse any argument before it has a chance to be heard or to intimidate those who might disagree with them into silence. Mel, who is accusing Steven of being color-blind at the beginning of this chapter, is well on his way to becoming a bulldozer.

   Bulldozers are not subtle, and they can be loud and forceful or as intensely damaging as a laser. They will often protest that their remarks or behavior are nothing personal, even though when you are attacked by a bulldozer you feel thoroughly flattened. Bulldozers simply use any means to achieve an end. Their bad behavior may get them what they want in the short term, but it is seldom effective in the long term.

Reality television shows, such as *The Real Housewives*, thrive on conflict to entertain audiences. The producers of these shows make sure they are cast with plenty of bulldozers, volcanoes, and snipers.

2. **Volcanoes**, as the term implies, are always on the verge of exploding. Like bulldozers, they are hostile and aggressive, but when they blow up, they lose all control. They typically blame a problem on someone else then blow up at the person or persons they believe caused the problem. They shout, insult, stomp around, and otherwise express their extreme discontent. A volcano's behavior is usually due to low self-esteem and a feeling of being threatened, but knowing this does not help the person who ends up in the middle of the volcano's explosion.

   In an earlier example, Carlene was a volcano who exploded at her boyfriend for dating Gloria. Later, Carlene also behaved like a sniper.

3. **Snipers** don't bulldoze you or explode at you; they talk about you behind your back, as in the earlier example where Carlene spread rumors about Gloria. The sniper makes little jokes about you, criticizes your choice in clothes, and otherwise tries to embarrass you. Like Mel at the beginning of this chapter, snipers usually protest that they were just kidding after taking a gibe at you. They often get away with their behavior because no one wants others to believe that he or she can't take a joke.[3]

You can't change toxic people, but you can learn to deal with them. Some of the techniques for defusing another person's anger, as discussed earlier, may work, and here are a few suggestions from Mike Moore's manual, *Dealing With Difficult People,* and from motivational speaker Kerry L. Johnson for dealing with bulldozers and volcanoes:

- Stand up to them—literally. Stand at eye level or get them to sit down. Never let them stand over you while you are sitting.

When dealing with an angry person, it helps to take a moment to cool yourself down. While it is tempting to respond to anger or violence with more anger and violence, that will not lead to a successful resolution.

- Remain calm. Your first impulse may be to respond in kind, but this often leads to physical violence. Respect the person and let him or her know that you expect respect in return. Don't settle for anything less.
- Listen attentively. Don't argue or interrupt, just listen. When the person has begun to wind down, ask questions about his or her problem. Don't accuse the person of bad behavior during his or her tantrum. Try to draw him or her into a constructive discussion. This may defuse the explosion and help him or her to calm down.
- Look the person directly in the eye and respond assertively but without emotion or aggression. Don't accuse or judge the person; just calmly tell him or her how you feel. If the person interrupts you, say, "Just a moment. Please let me finish."
- If the bulldozer or volcano insists on continuing to bully you, just say, "I don't allow anyone to treat me this way." Then slowly and calmly walk away. It is also effective to calmly stare at the person during an attack, then, without a word, just turn and walk away.
- Document in writing your attempts to resolve the conflict. This is useful if the conflict escalates to involve school authorities or if you opt for peer mediation.

The sniper requires special handling that is different from the above tips for handling bulldozers and volcanoes. Don't respond to comments made anonymously that you hear through the grapevine, recommends Johnson. If a sniper attacks you in front of others under the guise of joking, ignore him or her. The sniper wants you to laugh at yourself so he or she can attack again with more venom.

Get the sniper alone and confront him or her about comments directed against you. If he or she says, "Can't you take a joke?" say, "Sure, I can take a joke, but what you said about me sounded as though you weren't kidding. Did you mean to sound the way you did?" If the person says yes, you may discover what the real reason is behind the sniping.[4]

Handling difficult people takes skill and practice. You do not have to take all the grief they dish out; you can confront them. But remember that hostile arguments or violence are never the solution. It takes courage to confront problem people, and you cannot change them. You may, however, change the way they behave toward you.

If all else fails, you may have to separate yourself from the problem person in your life.

If you can make the above tips work for you, the difficult people in your life will no longer have control or influence over your emotions, behavior, or goals.

Do not be surprised if you have recognized your own behavior in any of the examples mentioned. We have all probably been the difficult person in the lives of others at one time or another. Maybe worries about an ill family member have made a person grumpy and uncooperative. Or perhaps a person is simply tired, and it requires too much energy to cooperate on a project. Maybe the easiest response to a request or a conflict seems to be to say and do nothing—another form of behavior that can irritate others.

There are reasons behind most disagreeable or annoying behavior, but most of us do not have the expertise to get to the source. We can only learn how to deal with the person's behavior to accomplish whatever goal is at hand or to resolve a conflict that will make life easier for all concerned.

7

From Conflict to Collaboration

Finding oneself in the midst of a disturbing argument may feel like being tossed inside a wave at the beach. You temporarily lose your sense of orientation and don't know which way to swim to take a breath. The route to conflict resolution often seems unclear, especially when emotions are running high. However, you can find your way beyond the turmoil by staying calm and making efforts to communicate more effectively.

You probably knew what arguments were before you opened this book—at least you knew that you had experienced them. Now that you have reached the last chapter of the book, you have no doubt gained some insight into how arguments develop and how to resolve them so that they do not dominate your emotions, decisions, and goals. As you practice the suggestions for satisfactorily resolving conflicts, you should notice a steady increase in self-esteem and self-confidence. In addition, you should notice an improvement in relationships that you consider important because difficult conflicts no longer keep you on edge around certain people.

As mentioned earlier, face-to-face communication is more likely to get your message across. This is true because the person you address can see your facial expressions and body language and can hear your tone of voice. For example, the comment, "So, you messed up again," is taken as the playful gibe it is meant to be if you are smiling when you say it and lightly jab the other person's arm.

On the other hand, if you scowl, raise your voice, and say, "So! You messed up again," the person to whom you are speaking will understandably deduce that you are angry.

E-mail and Texting as Sources of Conflict

This is why e-mail and texting, those universal methods of communicating that are now so pervasive in our lives, can so easily cause conflict. Since we usually think of conflicts as arising through face-to-face interaction, most of this resource has discussed these types of conflicts. But electronic messages are proving to be sources of conflict unique to the Internet age.

No doubt when e-mail programs were written, the creators envisioned a speedy method of communication that would give computer users time for more important workplace tasks. Unfortunately, e-mail has also created a high-tech source of conflict.

"We were friends until we started e-mailing while I was out of town last summer," says Jean, a high school freshman talking about her difficulties with a former friend. "Now we hardly speak to each other."

The problem was that Tiffany, Jean's friend, sent the following e-mail message to Jean, "Don't worry, Jean, Kent [Jean's boyfriend] is having fun while you are gone." Jean took the message to mean that Kent was dating others while she was out of town, and she thought Tiffany was gloating. Jean was angry, and she asked Tiffany what was going on.

E-mailing, texting, and social media are convenient methods of communication, but it can be difficult to interpret some messages without understanding the writer's tone and intention. Before taking a text message the wrong way, read it a few times.

Tiffany tried to explain that she meant that Kent was not having fun, but she had failed to point out that she was being sarcastic, and Jean took it at face value. Jean conjured scenarios about Tiffany stealing her boyfriend, and the friendship cooled. The moral is that it is difficult to get sarcasm or other emotions across without tone of voice and facial expressions.

Business users of e-mail have also found it to be fast but sometimes confusing. "If you are in a hurry," says Dave, a self-employed accountant, "an e-mail message can come across as the exact opposite of what you meant." For example, he sent a message to a client to bring in additional records for income tax preparation, and the message seemed so abrupt that the client was insulted. The message read, "I need more documentation re. your business entertainment deduction ASAP." The client somehow interpreted this to mean that Dave did not trust him or questioned his business deductions, and he was huffy when he delivered the requested records.

As texting has become a common form of interpersonal communication, similar problems have arisen. When the person you are communicating with cannot see you or hear your voice, it is easy to misinterpret the message. Here are some tips to keep your e-mails and texts from becoming high-tech arguments:

1. Reread your e-mail messages or texts before sending them out to prevent creating unintentional conflicts.
2. Use emoticons (smiley faces) to represent your emotional state—but only in your personal messages to friends. Smileys are not appropriate to include in messages to businesses, employers, colleges, teachers, or in other more formal situations. Most e-mail programs and cell phones offer a choice of emoticons, or you can create your own using parentheses, the colon, semicolon, dash, and other punctuation marks. Some examples include:

Emoticons can go a long way toward making your meaning clear when sending an e-mail or text message. Sometimes words are not enough.

:-) = "I'm smiling." (happy, not sad or angry)

;-) = "I'm winking." (kidding)

:-(= "I'm angry/sad."

:-o = "I'm shocked/surprised."

:-@ = "I'm screaming." (denotes outrage)

:-I = "I'm indifferent." (denotes that you don't care)

:-e = "I'm disappointed."

>:-/ = "I'm angry."

:-D = "I'm laughing."

:-$ = "Put your money where your mouth is."

:-P = "I'm sticking out my tongue."

Emoticons give the person at the receiving end of the message some idea of your state of mind so conflicts can be avoided.

3. LOL after a statement or question means laugh out loud and can indicate that you were teasing or that you take the statement lightly and were not serious. It is annoying when overused, but when used sparingly and honestly, it can also indicate that your message is intended to be taken lightly.
4. Ask for clarification of the meaning of an e-mail message or text you have received before you jump to the conclusion that the message is insulting or otherwise undesirable. Ask questions such as, "Did you mean that . . . , or is this what you meant . . . ?"

E-mail has also been used as a bully's weapon since threats can be leveled with anonymity and without face-to-face contact. Victims of cyberbullies should print copies of such poisonous messages as proof of the abuse in case charges are brought.

Adjust Your Attitude

If you find yourself constantly embroiled in arguments with others, maybe you need to ask yourself if you need to change your attitude. For example, in *Getting What You Want: How to Reach Agreement and Resolve Conflict Every Time*, author Kare Anderson asks:

1. Do you make assumptions about people based on certain personal characteristics, such as the way they dress? For example, "Do you assume that the new kid will be uncooperative because she's wearing a black leather skirt, spiked hair, and purple lipstick?" Anderson suggests that this person "may be the computer whiz" who can show you how to do new and amazing things on the computer.
2. Do you mark someone who doesn't initiate a conversation as unfriendly? "He may be painfully shy," Anderson advises.
3. Do you take advantage of someone who seems always cheerfully ready to help with your projects? That person, writes Anderson, "may be saying scathing things about you to half the people" you know.[1]

Anderson and other experts also warn against making assumptions about people based on certain behavior, such as:

- Smoking (Assumption: They must be stupid.)
- Weird clothes (They must be clueless.)
- Putting on makeup in public (They must be shallow airheads.)
- Dressing expensively (Their parents must be rich.)

Assumptions can lead to conflict if you slight others or otherwise treat them differently because of assumptions you have made. Assumptions are not necessarily bad, and we all make them, Anderson writes, "They just aren't very good barometers if you really

Avoid making snap judgements about other people based solely on their looks. That goth kid across the room has a distinct personality that you can't possibly know unless you talk to him.

want to know and honor the truth about another person, or if you want accurate information on which to base action or negotiation."[2]

Send Yourself Positive Messages

When you speak purposefully to yourself, advise Brinkman and Kirschner in *Dealing With People You Can't Stand,* you can change your attitude toward difficult people for the better:

1. Accept the situation for what it is. That doesn't mean that you have to take abuse from someone, but if you constantly struggle with a conflict or withdraw, you will remain frustrated. When you see the situation realistically, your chances of resolving a conflict improve.
2. Try to see the conflict as an opportunity—perhaps to improve a relationship or to develop your conflict resolution skills.
3. Examine your experiences with difficult people to see what you have learned. Are you stronger because of the experience? Did you learn more about yourself from the experience? What is working in dealing with a difficult person in your life, and what is not?
4. Be flexible. Try other novel approaches when it is clear that your methods of dealing with a difficult person are not working now and will probably never work.
5. Let conflict surface when it exists, but if you simply can't find a solution, perhaps the best attitude is, "Oh well, I can't change this person, but I can change the way I react."[3]

The tips and techniques you have learned up to this point should help you resolve arguments with others when they arise and possibly even avoid arguments in a satisfactory manner. Two final facts to remember, however, are:

Conflict does not have to be a bad thing; it can actually bring people closer. If you get into arguments that are not hurtful and instead are productive, you can learn a lot about other people.

- You are not likely to change the person with whom you are in disagreement.
- Conflicts in your life will not always be resolved in your favor.

When you run up against one or both of these truths, you can let anger simmer and make you miserable, or you can tell yourself that you did everything you could do and move on with your life. In any event, the skills you learn for conflict resolution will help ensure that you always make the best decisions for handling arguments wisely.

Remember: every argument presents an opportunity for growth. Whether at home, in school, in the workplace, or wherever you go in life, having some solid strategies for dealing with arguments as they arise will ease your passage, serve as an example to others, and help you evolve as a person.

Chapter Notes

Chapter 1: Defining Conflict

1. Tim Ursiny, Ph.D., *The Coward's Guide to Conflict: Empowering Solutions for Those Who Would Rather Run Than Fight* (Naperville, Ill.: Sourcebooks, Inc., 2003), p. xix.
2. Brad Evens, *Types of Conflict: Four Classifications,* August 16, 2013, < http://www.typesofconflict.org> (June 22, 2015).
3. Mediate.com University, n.d., <http://www.mediate.com/divorce/pg17.cfm> (June 22, 2015).
4. David W. Johnson and Roger T. Johnson, *Reducing School Violence Through Conflict Resolution* (Alexandria, Va.: Association for Supervision and Curriculum Development, 1995), pp. 16–17.
5. Ibid., p. 17.
6. Peers Making Peace, program profile, n.d., <https://www.crimesolutions.gov/ProgramDetails.aspx?ID=329> (June 22, 2015).
7. "About Us," *Operation Respect: Don't Laugh at Me,* n.d., <http://www.operationrespect.org> (June 19, 2015).
8. Stacy Teicher Khadaroo, *Christian Science Monitor,* "Restorative justice: one high school's path to reducing suspensions by half," March 31, 2013 <http://www.csmonitor.com/USA/Education/2013/0331/Restorative-justice-One-high-school-s-path-to-reducing-suspensions-by-half> (June 19, 2015).
9. Stewart Levine, *Getting to Resolution: Turning Conflict into Collaboration* (San Francisco: Berrett-Koehler Publishers, Inc., 1998), pp. xii–xiii.

Chapter 2: Arguments Happen

1. Kenneth W. Thomas and Ralph H. Kilmann, "An Overview of the Thomas-Kilmann Conflict Mode Instrument", n.d., <http://www.kilmanndiagnostics.com/overview-thomas-kilmann-conflict-mode-instrument-tki> (June 22, 2015).
2. Kare Anderson, *Getting What You Want: How to Reach Agreement and Resolve Conflict Every Time* (New York: Dutton, 1993), pp. 155–156.
3. Gary Harper, *The Joy of Conflict Resolution: Transforming Victims, Villains and Heroes in the Workplace and at Home* (Gabriola Island, British Columbia, Canada: New Society Publishers, 2004), pp. 74–81.
4. Anderson, p 159.

Chapter 3: Resolving Conflicts and Reducing Arguments

1. Luis Miguel Diaz, "Animal Behavior as a Source for Unlearning and Relearning Strategies for Conflict Prevention and Resolution," Mediate.com, July 2008, <http://www.mediate.com/articles/diaz9.cfm> (June 23, 2015).
2. "How to Avoid Causing Offence," Happiness Weekly, July 16, 2012, <http://happinessweekly.org/2012/07/16/how-to-avoid-causing-offence/> (June 22, 2015).
3. "Making Peace: Tips on Managing Conflict," n.d., <http://www.healthieryou.com/manconflict.html> (June 22, 2015).
4. "Active Listening," *Coaching Center*, n.d., <http://www.gocampus.org/modx/index.php?id=157> (June 22, 2015).
5. "What Is Bullying?" n.d., <http://www.stopbullying.gov/what-is-bullying/> (June 16, 2015) and "Jared's Story," n.d., <http://www. jaredstory.com> (June 16, 2015).
6. *Bully Police USA*, n.d., <http://www.bullypolice.org> (June 21, 2015).

7. National Bullying Prevention Center, June 1, 2015, <http://www.pacer.org/bullying/stories>(June 21, 2015).
8. Ibid.
9. Author's interview with Jordan Valacich, November 12, 2004.
10. Elizabeth Bennett, "Peer Abuse Know More," n.d., <http://www.peerabuse.net> (June 22, 2015).

Chapter 4: Problems and Solutions

1. David W. Johnson and Roger T. Johnson, *Reducing School Violence Through Conflict Resolution* (Alexandria, Va.: Association for Supervision and Curriculum Development, 1995), p. 52.
2. Human Resources Department, University of Wisconsin, Madison, Wisconsin, "Managing Impasse," n.d., <https://www.ohrd.wisc.edu/onlinetraining/resolution/commonproblems.htm> (June 22, 2015).
3. Youth Activism Project, "Success Stories," n.d., <http://youthactivismproject.org/success-stories> (June 20, 2015).
4. Ibid.
5. *BBC News*, "Malala Yousafzai: A Profile," December 10, 2014, <http://www.bbc.com/news/world-asia-23241937> (June 18, 2015).
6. Shalu Bhalla, ed., *Quotes of M.K. Gandhi* (New Delhi, India: UBS Publishers Distributors, 1995), p. 1.
7. The Hero File: Archbishop Desmond Mpilo Tutu, September 10, 2014, <http://www.moreorless.net.au/heroes/tutu.html> (June 22, 2015).
8. Ibid.
9. Ibid.
10. M.K. Gandhi: Excerpts and Quotations, n.d., <http://www.quietspaces.com/gandhiquotes.html> (June 22, 2015).

Chapter 5: How Peer Mediation Works

1. Ruth Perlstein and Gloria Thrall, *Ready-to-Use Conflict Resolution Activities for Secondary Students* (San Francisco: Jossey-Bass, 1996), pp. 117–118.
2. Ibid., p. 152.

Chapter 6: Difficult Personality Types

1. Rick Brinkman and Rick Kirschner, *Dealing With People You Can't Stand: How to Bring Out the Best in People at Their Worst*, 3rd ed. (New York: McGraw-Hill, 2012).
2. Mike Moore, *The Art of Verbal Self-defense: Dealing with Difficult People*, 2011, <http://www.motivationalplus.com/media/The_Art_of_Verbal_Self_Defense.pdf> (June 22, 2015).
3. Kerry L. Johnson, Ph.D., "Coping With Problem People," n.d., <http://www.kerryjohnson.com/index12.php?page=problem_people.html> (June 22, 2015).
4. Ibid.; and Moore.

Chapter 7: From Conflict to Collaboration

1. Kare Anderson, *Getting What You Want: How to Reach Agreement and Resolve Conflict Every Time* (New York: Penguin Group, 1994), pp. 60–61.
2. Ibid., p. 61.
3. Rick Brinkman and Rick Kirschner, *Dealing With People You Can't Stand: How to Bring Out the Best in People at Their Worst*, 3rd ed. (New York: McGraw-Hill, 2012.

Glossary

accommodation—Giving in to the needs and wishes of others.

alternative dispute resolution—Using mediation or arbitration to avoid taking a case to court.

anger management—Learning to recognize signs that you're becoming angry and taking action to calm down and deal with the situation in a positive way.

arbitration—Settling a dispute through a neutral third party who has the power to make decisions that are binding to both sides.

avoidance—Solving a conflict by walking away from it.

conflict resolution—Techniques for settling a disagreement with another person, group, or within one's self.

denial—Solving a conflict by pretending it does not exist.

intergroup—Between two or more groups.

interpersonal—Between people.

intragroup—Within a group.

intrapersonal—Within one's self.

mediation—Settling a dispute through a neutral third party who does not have the power to make binding decisions.

negotiation—To discuss something in order to reach an agreement.

peer abuse—Bullying.

peer mediation—A process by which two or more students involved in a dispute meet to work out problems with the help of a trained student mediator.

reconciliation—Settling a conflict between opposing individuals or groups and restoring peace.

restorative justice—A system that focuses on rehabilitating offenders through reconciliation with victims and the community. In school settings, restorative justice is used to settle disputes between students.

For More Information

Alliance for Conflict Transformation
PO Box 9117
Alexandria, VA 22304
(703) 879-7039
www.conflicttransformation.org

Changing Children's Worlds Foundation
411 Stevens Street
Geneva, IL 60134
(630) 909-9411
www.changingchildrensworlds.org

Peace Learning Center
6040 Delong Rd.
Indianapolis, IN 46254
(317) 327-7144
peacelearningcenter.org

Stop Bullying
200 Independence Avenue SW
Washington, DC 20201
(800) 273-TALK
www.stopbullying.gov

Youth Leadership Institute
28 Second Street, Suite 400
San Francisco, CA 94105
(415) 836-9160
www.yli.org

Websites

CRInfo: Conflict Resolution Information Source

crinfo.org

Clearinghouse for conflict resolution resources

National Bully Police

bullypolice.org

Watchdog website providing information on state anti-bullying laws

Operation Respect

operationrespect.org

Non-profit organization dedicated to creating safe, respectful, bully-free schools

Students Against Violence Everywhere (SAVE)

nationalsave.org

Non-profit organization promoting student involvement in decreasing the potential for violence in schools

Further Reading

Buttry, Daniel L. *Blessed Are the Peacemakers*. Canton, Mich.: David Crumm Media, 2011.

Crutcher, Chris. *Angry Management: Three Novellas*. New York: Greenwillow Books, 2011.

Doeden, Matt. *Conflict Resolution Smarts: How to Communicate, Negotiate, Compromise, and More* (USA Today Teen Wise Guides). Minneapolis, Minn.: Lerner Publishing Group, 2012.

Katri, Vikhas. *Nobel Peace Prize Winners: People Who Worked for a Noble Cause*. New Delhi, India: V&S Publishers, 2012.

Smith, Marilyn E., et al. *School Violence and Conflict Resolution*. New York: Rosen Publishing Group, 2012.

Stiehm, Judith Hicks. *Champions for Peace: Women Winners of the Nobel Peace Prize*. Lanham, Md.: Rowman & Littlefield Publishers, 2013.

Index

D

E

F

G

H

I

T

U

V

W

Y